Broken Engagement - Joan's Story

ESTHER THOMSON SMITH

FIRST Edition – Copyright © 1998
Second Edition – Merged into
THIRD Edition -- Copyright © 1999
Fourth Edition– Merged into
FIFTH Edition – Copyright © 2013
Copyrights by Esther Thomson Smith
With Library of Congress Catalog Card Numbers

All Rights Reserved

Paperback book
ISBN-13: 9781493613557
ISBN-10: 1493613553

E-Book ISBN: 978-0-615-88588-9

This book is available for purchase
As an E-BOOK at Kindle.com
And as a PAPERBACK BOOK from
CreateSpace eStore (CreateSpace.com/4501803)
And from Amazon.com
As well as from other retailers.

Printed in the United States of America

DEDICATION

To my daughter, with love

To my long-time dear friend
Diana Tiongco

With best wishes for your health,
happiness and sense of inner
serenity.

Love,
Esther Thomson Smith
'74

BROKEN ENGAGEMENT
JOAN'S STORY

Fifth Edition

PROLOGUE

Ding-dong, ding-dong, ding-dong went the front door bell. There was a pause, followed by more insistent ringing. Joan hurried from the kitchen. She glanced out of the living room window and seeing Clara Clark's car, unlocked the front door, unlatched the screen door, and opened her arms to her crying oldest granddaughter.

After a few minutes, Clara lifted her head from Joan's shoulder. "Grandma, I knew I could come talk with you. Nobody's home. I just 'ave to talk with someone. I couldn't wait until later! I need to talk NOW! I feel like I'm going to explode!"

Just then, a ding, ding, ding sounded. Startled, Joan said, "I need to take something out of the oven. Let's go into the kitchen 'n you can tell me what happened." Joan turned slowly with her arm around Clara, and the two of them walked from the living room, through the hall and on towards the dinging sound. Soon Clara was sitting in her usual chair by the kitchen table as Joan whiffed the air and hurried towards the oven.

Clara sniffled and then said, "Bob—we 'ad a big fight. In the end, he broke our engagement. He said he doesn't 'ave a drinking problem. I've no right to interfere with his seeing his friends and 'aving a few drinks with them. He doesn't want to marry me 'n get strongly criticized the rest of his life. No, forget about it! He's finished with me. He ended up shouting and shaking his finger in my face. But, he does get angry easily when he's drunk. He's even hit me a few times when he's that way. I love him, and I thought he loved me enough to change. He shoved me aside, pushing me so 'ard that I landed on the floor. He didn't even turn to check on me before he tramped to the front door and slammed it! The slam was so 'ard that it shook the wall so much that Mom's favorite photograph on the hall wall fell to the floor. The glass protecting the picture shattered and broke into a million pieces." Clara wiped her eyes.

Joan pulled a pan of nearly overdone cookies from the oven and placed some on a plate on the table. She filled two tall glasses with Clara's favorite drink, a rich blend of cold fruit juice that Joan always kept on hand. Then, the white haired grandmother sat at the table in a chair opposite her nineteen year old redheaded granddaughter. She reached her hand towards Clara with an expression of sympathy on her face.

"I know, honey," Joan said. "You feel like your world has come to an end. What you thought was permanent—well, just isn't. There's a spot inside that hurts so much you want to tear it out. The sharp pain feels like it's never going to end. Dying would be a relief."

Clara looked surprised. "You do understand. You really do! Did you 'ave a broken engagement, too?"

"Broken engagements don't always stay broken, but many do. Each situation is different." Joan stopped to nibble on a cookie. "My engagement was broken when I was nineteen, just as you are now. Would you like to hear the story?

Clara smiled, much to her grandmother's relief. "Oh, yes, I'd love to hear about it." Clara leaned forward in anticipation. Neither noticed that outside a gentle rain had started falling. It was warm and cozy in the kitchen.

Joan sighed. "I've never told this story to anyone before, but I think now is the time. My story begins years ago on what I still call *Terrible Tuesday.*"

1

"Oh, what a beautiful morning," sang happy me, Joan Alexander, as I fingered the engagement ring wonderful Richard Seymour had given me the night before. He was coming again tonight, and we'd discuss plans about our future together. I petted my long-haired white cat, Fluffy, before opening the door to leave for my early Tuesday morning college class. Even the weather was good this day—clear, without the normal seasonal fog. This second Tuesday of November was going to be a great day, I just knew it.

Within an hour, I was going to realize that prediction was so wrong, Wrong, very WRONG! It turned out to become what I still call *Terrible Tuesday*.

I drove my compact car to the college. Actually, it was and still is classified as a being a university. The large campus accommodates over fifteen thousand students. I was lucky the university was within twenty miles of my home. I was studying to become an elementary school teacher. There were several student parking lots, but it was less walking distance if I could park on a street closer to the buildings where my classes were being held. As it turned out, I'd left home a little later than usual. I hoped my favorite parking place would still be available. It was close to the building where my first morning class this Tuesday was located. Another student and I seemed to race for that spot. Most of the cars were too big to fit there.

Drat! I couldn't use the small parking space sandwiched between two driveways. Attached to a white sawhorse across "my" space was a CLOSED FOR

REPAIRS sign. I decided to go further down the street to see if I could find an empty spot. It was then that I noticed my friend, Tom Jensen, waving his arms and pointing. *Yes, oh my yes, there's an empty parking space!* I drove my little Ladybug, as I called my red car, into the spot. On the right side was a blue car and on the left was a long dirty black van with its double side doors open. A man was placing a metal folding chair into the van. As he did so, I noticed a paper with the word RESERVED taped to the back of the chair.

I reached for my book bag and my oversized purse on the seat next to me. Then, I pulled the key on the key ring out of the ignition. Tom stood by my car door when I opened it. He pushed a strand of brown hair away from his face. Normally, he would have offered to carry my books. I could tell Tom liked me very much. It showed in how his hazel eyes grew tender when he looked into mine. He'd asked me to go with him to a college dance recently. He was disappointed when I told him no because I was going steady with someone else. His left eyebrow and the small mole beside it near his nose seemed to wiggle with emotion. Obviously, he had been deeply disappointed. And yet, he seemed always to be there waiting for me when I arrived those mornings when we both had early classes. Yes, Tom was very fond of me. I knew that for certain.

"I've an appointment with my counselor first thing this morning," Tom told me. "In fact," he added, "I'm a bit late for it now. Sorry, I'd better rush off. See yah later." He turned and hurriedly walked away. I saw his face had turned pale when he noticed my engagement ring. I had a feeling that he had made up an excuse to leave.

I closed the car door and started to lock it. Just then, the man jumped down from the open doors of the van and bumped into me. The jarring caused me to drop my keys. They slid under the car just behind the front left wheel.

"Oh, sorry," the man mumbled. "Least I cin do is tah git the keys for yah." With that, he squeezed past me in a not-very-gentle way and leaned over to retrieve my keys. Something made me feel uneasy. It was like the hairs on the back of my neck were vibrating. My nerves were on edge. Why did I feel a sense of danger?

When the man stood and turned towards me holding out the key ring, I looked at him more closely. He had long black hair and a big bushy beard of the same color. His clothes looked old and too large for his frame. The hat on his head had a wide brim and his dark glasses made seeing his eyes difficult. Why would a person wear dark sunglasses this early in the morning?

I reached for the offered keys. Suddenly, the man grabbed my wrist and pushed and pulled me towards the open side doors of the van. I was so startled, I didn't think about screaming or yelling for help. Before I realized what had happened, I found myself inside the back of the van. My book bag followed by my purse plunked down on the van floor. The man pushed a smelly cloth over my face. Then I was on the floor too. I felt weak and disoriented. I was only vaguely aware of who I was. I shook my head and tried to recapture reality.

By then, the smelly thing over my nose and mouth was gone. I found myself in a prone position with my back towards something soft. I had a gag in my mouth secured to my face with some sort of wide tape. My hands were fastened together in front of me with something pulling my elbows towards the cold floor of the van. I couldn't move my feet. They seemed to be tied together and then fastened to the floor. I noticed the van doors were closed, and I was totally helpless!

"That'll hold you 'til we git tah where we're goin', Cutie," the bearded man said menacingly. "Because we have a long way tah go, I decided not tah tie your hands behind your back. I hope you appreciate not havin' tah lay with the weight of your back pressin' down on your hands 'n arms mile after mile. Now, I'm gonna place the paint-spotted canvas over yah tah keep you warm. It'll hide your body too should anybody happen tah look in here. 'N tah hide the rest of you, I've got a cardboard box with holes punched in the sides tah place over your head. Aren't I smart? Got the whole thin' figured out down tah the last detail."

With the gag in my mouth, I couldn't reply. Something in my mouth under the tape made breathing more difficult. I was very uncomfortable lying there and unable to move more than an inch in any direction. I stared at the man with a frosty angry glare, and the man grinned. "Cat got your tongue, huh? Can't say what you're thinkin'? Wal, wait until we git tah where we're goin' 'n, if'n you dare, I'll bet you'd have plenty tah say tah me or wish you could. I'm lookin' forward tah your reactions when we git tah the lonely mountain cabin." He chuckled.

I'd never been so frightened in my whole life. I was totally at his mercy. What did he have in mind to do with me? Was he going to rape and then kill me? Both of my parents and my older brother had died in an auto accident last December.

My parents had life insurance, and it was enough to pay for my living and college expenses until I was able to graduate and earn a living. Surely, ransom wasn't the motive for this kidnapping. Was this the random snatching of a female, or did he intend to capture me specifically? Was the sign across "my" parking spot placed there to lure me next to the van? Had the chair with the reserved sign been placed to save the parking spot just for me? If it was a plot, how come Tom helped lure me to it? He cared about me. He wouldn't knowingly be a part of a dire plot to harm me. Of that I was positive. Oh, what was going to happen next? I wasn't sure I wanted to know.

I sensed when the man moved to the front seat of the van. Then I heard the engine start. Loud country music blared from the radio. I felt the motion when the man got out of the vehicle. He was talking with someone, but I couldn't hear what was being said. He was humming to the tune on the radio when he returned to the front seat. He turned the volume down. "Wal, I gave your keys tah someone who'll move your car. He'll pick up your mail 'n feed your cat. He'll tell your nosey neighbor that you'd hired him tah mow your lawn 'n take care of your place while you're away. An emergency came up 'n you had tah leave suddenly. Told you I'd figured everythin' out tah the last detail."

I moaned. So, he had deliberately snatched me, not just any girl who happened to come along. He had made plans ahead of time to prevent my neighbor from becoming suspicious about my absence. It sounded like he expected I'd be gone from home for days—or would it be longer? Why?

The van moved for what seemed like a very long time. My arms ached and so did my back. My right leg got a cramp that finally went away. The van stopped once. The man politely told me he had to refuel, but oh yes, he had filled gas cans and could do it himself without going to a service station. See, he added, he'd planned everything down to the smallest detail. Soon the van was moving again.

I needed to go to the bathroom. I was thirsty and hungry. Scared too! I was still helplessly fastened to the floor of the van. Why me? What good could I do for the bearded man? If rape was his purpose, could I somehow convince him that I'd be worth keeping alive to satisfy his sexual wants? Could I pretend to fall in love with him? What were my options? Yes, I needed to figure out options. I couldn't do that until I learned more about where we were going and what was in store for me there. Would I ever see my dear Richard again? He was the only surviving child of wealthy parents. Could my kidnapping be for ransom from them?

I must have fallen asleep. I became aware that the van had stopped. The music was turned off. I felt motion at the back of the vehicle. The box was removed from over my head. I blinked up at my captor. He had removed his sunglasses and was grinning at me. "Wal, Cutie, we've arrived. Let me help yah up 'n then I'll show you the cabin." There was gleam in his eyes that scared me. I had a feeling that what I could expect in that cabin wasn't going to be pleasant—pleasant for me anyway. I knew I could expect more misery.

When I was standing with my feet freed from their bonds and my elbows released from being held down, I looked and saw tie-down places here and there on the vehicle's floor. I noted there was a folded blanket where I'd been. I wasn't allowed to observe much before I was guided to the van's open side doors and gently lifted to the ground. I looked around to see my new surroundings. We were in a forested area of low hills with several types of trees including oaks and what I thought were cedars. There were no mountains in sight. A path led up a slight slope to a rustic looking old cabin with a wide covered front porch. After closing the van's doors, the man grabbed my left arm with a firm grip and proceeded to lead me up the path towards the cabin. Although my feet were free, my hands were still bound in front of me, and the gag was still in place. I looked around wildly. It appeared the cabin was in an isolated area. Even if I yelled loudly for help, no one would hear me. The sun was setting. We'd been traveling for hours. Dusk was not far away. As the man guided me up the path, my legs felt like sticks, and I walked very carefully, step by cautious step. My arms ached and so did my back. A squirrel with a bushy tail scooted out of our way as we headed towards the cabin.

"Be careful of those tree roots over the path," the man said. I looked and stepped over them. "Pretty place, huh?" He paused. "Oh, you can't talk with that gag. You sure don't need it here. There's nobody for miles 'n we are at the end of a little used dirt road. You won't be seein' any cars passing by here." He pulled the tape from my face, and something from my mouth went too. Obviously, he had thought of a way to place something inside my mouth and to secure it so I wouldn't choke. Yes, he had been very thorough with his planning. "Better?" he asked. My face hurt where the tape had been. At least now I could breathe better. That was a big relief! Deciding (in slang terms) *to play it cool*, I replied, "Yes. Thank you."

Soon we were up the cabin steps. When we were on the porch, the man unlocked the screen door. He turned and gave me what seemed like a nasty smile. "Almost in what will be your new home," he said gleefully. "We made it here safely." He unlocked the main front door. I noticed there were bars over the two big front windows and over the screen door too. It reminded me of a prison. The bearded man shoved me inside the cabin, and I blinked. There were drapes over the windows, and it was dark in there. *I'm scared! What's going to happen next?*

2

The room looked cozy once the man flipped the electric light switch. It was a combination kitchen-living room. A door led to a hall. I could see that much before I was suddenly pushed onto a wooden chair next to an old fashioned wooden dining room table. My back was towards the kitchen sink, stove and refrigerator. I barely caught my breath from the sudden landing on the chair when I realized the man was pulling a leather belt around my waist and fastening it behind the rungs at the back of the chair. Next, he tied my shoe laces to the front legs of the chair. My hands were still bound in front of me. I was his prisoner as much as I had been in the van. My need to go to the bathroom was getting more acute by the minute.

"Wal now, Cutie, seems it's jest you 'n me. Yeh cin call me Mike. That doesn't have tah be my right name, but you cin call me that. We're goin' tah git tah know each other real well in the next few days. Doesn't that sound interestin'?" He gave me a wide grin. I shivered involuntarily, and he saw it. "So you're scared of me, are you? Wal, that's good. I even have the strap my dad used tah whip me with when I was naughty. I hope I don't have tah use it on you."

My head was spinning. I needed to get away from this topic. Hopefully, maybe I could do that by changing the subject. My voice cracked when I said, "Mike, I really, really need to go to the bathroom."

Mike studied me carefully before deciding to accommodate me. After the belt at my waist was removed and my feet were freed, I was taken through the door to the hall, turned left and then into a bedroom with bunk beds. I was pointed towards another door and told it was the bathroom. My hands were still bound in front of me. Once alone in the bathroom, I managed to used the facilities. It occurred to me then that slacks instead of the skirt I almost wore that day turned out to be a good choice. When I was again properly dressed, I leaned my head down to the sink faucet to take a long drink of cold refreshing water. I turned on the faucet, but no water came out. No water? I'd just flushed the toilet, but didn't hear the tank refilling. Well, it wasn't my problem just then. I hated the idea of facing Mike again. There was only one exit out of the room. I couldn't stall there very long or he'd come checking to find out why. I really had no choice. I opened the door and faced my captor. In his right hand, he held a pocket knife with the blade exposed. I gulped—twice! Now what was going to happen?

"I've been thinkin'," Mike told me. "There's no reason tah keep your hands tied while here in the cabin. I warn you, though, not tah threaten me in any way. 'N not tah try leavin' the cabin unless I tell you." He snarled at me, "If'n you do, you won't live tah see another day. Understood?"

"Yesssss," I answered in a broken voice. He was frightening me worse than I'd been before. I believed he could kill me and to him it would be like swatting a fly.

A few minutes later with my hands free and my feet too, I was seated at the table while Mike heated a kettle with pork and beans from a can and a water filled teakettle on the stove. We ended up with big cups of hot tea and warm pork and beans with crackers. I felt starved. I hadn't eaten or had anything to drink since breakfast and that was hours ago. What was placed in front of me looked really special and tasted even better!

While Mike was studying me, I looked around the room. The floor looked to be constructed of unfinished wide pine planks. If it had ever been waxed, it was a long time ago. A year old calendar with a picture of three kittens in a basket was the only decoration on the walls. Unless, that is, a person considered the kerosene lamp on its own shelf above the sofa a decoration. The lamp's glass chimney had a pattern of what looked to me like an etching and was prettier than the plain kerosene lamp my grandmother had years ago. Where the drapes were partly open, I noticed bars on the small widow over the kitchen sink. I saw a brick fireplace in the corner of the west and south walls. It had an elevated brick hearth. I noticed cobwebs hanging down from the ceiling in parts of the room. I discovered more cobwebs under the table. Ugh! I stopped surveying the room when Mike spoke.

"I'm goin' tah let you sleep in the bedroom we went through on your way tah the bathroom. My two sisters used tah have that room. You are free tah use whatever you see in the dresser or closet. Since you'll be here for awhile, you'll need a change of clothes. You are a bit smaller than my youngest sister, but at least you'll have somethin' tah wear. You cin wash clothes in the bathroom 'n hang them tah dry on the foldin' rack you'll find stored under the bottom bunk bed. My sisters used tah place the rack when in use inside the bathtub. You cin use anythin' you find in the bathroom too. I think there's a package of new toothbrushes in the drawer. You must stay in those quarters my sisters used until I knock on your door in the mornin'. Git up now, let's go."

I soon found myself alone in the bedroom. I wasn't really surprised when I heard the click of the bedroom door being locked behind me. When I checked to see what options for escaping there might be, I again noticed bars covered the windows---a single bedroom window and a small one in the bathroom. The bars seemed to be on sort of swinging doors fastened on the outside of the window moldings. The hinges faced the room. There were stout metal rings on the opposite side from the hinges at the top and bottom of each bar door. Each metal ring was held firmly in place by a padlock. I looked closer and discovered the hinges and the padlocks were of the security type, and this prevented an unauthorized successful tampering of them. Trying to escape through a bedroom or bathroom window would be useless.

Later that night in one of the nightgowns from a dresser drawer, I lay wide awake. I was under the blankets on the lower bunk bed. I wondered what was in store for me the next day. What was Richard going to think when he came to see me at seven o'clock that night, and I wasn't there? Would he go next door to ask Mrs. Connor if she had any idea where I was? She was known in the neighborhood as being very nosey, but everyone liked her anyway. *Oh, Richard, I love you so much!* Hours later, I cried myself to sleep.

■ ■ ■

The rap-rap-rap on the door awoke me. I opened my eyes. Sunlight brightened the room. The strange surroundings startled me until I remembered my circumstances. Then, my fears from last night echoed again in my thoughts. Best put on a good front, I decided. I sat up and hit my head on the lower part of the upper bunk. That hurt! I had laid a bathrobe over the chair by the bed the previous night. I had just finished donning it when the door opened. I faced the man who held me prisoner. "Git dressed," he ordered gruffly. "Then come eat breakfast. We've got a lot tah accomplish tahday." He turned, closed the door and left me. This is how what I call *Awful Wednesday* started.

I hurriedly put on my clothes from yesterday. While in the bathroom, I ran my fingers through my curly light brown hair. I checked in the mirror and decided I was lucky to have short hair at a time like this. I remembered years ago when I'd asked my mother why I had a different color of hair than any of the rest of my family. My mother was proud of her pretty red hair. My father and brother each had the same shade of dark black hair. Mom looked sad for just an instant before saying she'd wondered about that too. She said she'd looked at some old family pictures of both her ancestors and her husband's. Some of them showed lighter colored hair than others in the black and white prints of those days. She told me, "DNA works in strange ways sometimes. You've obviously inherited your hair color from someone. You have brown eyes like your father and brother, and high arches in your feet like mine. In case you ever think about it, I'm very definitely your mother. You are not an adopted child, and I love you very much."

I wondered why Mike was so cross this morning. What was it we had to accomplish today? I hesitated before entering the main room. I'd put off doing that as long as I'd dared. Assuming a brave front, I walked into the room and took my place at the table. Mike was sitting with a scowling expression on his face. Oh, this was not a good omen. I had judged him to be about thirty-five years old, but with his current expression he looked closer to forty. We had milk over canned peaches and corn flakes for breakfast. We had just emptied our bowls when the whistling teakettle started to shrill loudly. Mike got up. Once the flame on the stove was turned off, he began pouring hot water over tea bags in large cups placed on the counter. I took the opportunity to look under the table. I was relieved to see the spider webs were gone.

"What are you lookin' for?" Mike asked. He had turned towards the table while I had my head down. I sat up straight again before answering. "I wanted to see if there were any spiders in the webs. I was hoping if there were any, none of them would be black ones. I'm glad the webs are gone now."

Mike nodded his head. "You don't like spider webs 'n you especially don't like black spiders. Wal, never mind. Drink your tea."

With butterflies in my stomach, I dared to ask Mike why he had taken me prisoner. He looked at me a moment and then shrugged his shoulders. "Guess it doesn't matter if'n I tell you. Wal, it wasn't by mistake. I was hired tah do it. In fact, once I knew the person wanted me tah create a so-called accident that would end your life, I decided if'n I refused, she'd git someone else tah do it. Instead, I bargained with her. She finally agreed that if'n you did what she wanted, she'd let you live. Tah make certain her purposes were met, however, she made me take a solemn oath sayin' that if'n I couldn't persuade you tah do as she requires, I would follow through with the fatal 'accident' plan. I felt certain I could convince you, so I took the oath she demanded. It seemed the only way tah save your life."

I was silent as I absorbed what he had just said. I suspected he was fibbing. I decided to see how much more information I could learn. "How did she know how to find you? Are you a private detective or something?"

"Cutie, if'n I tell you all you want tah know, I'm placin' myself in your hands once you are free. It seems better tah keep some facts from you. But, if'n it ever comes tah pass that you need tah give a description of your kidnapper, I want you tah tell exactly what I look like now." I couldn't believe what I'd just heard. I studied him and decided Mike was quite serious.

"I could truthfully say you are about six feet tall, have long black hair and a bushy black beard. Let's see, you have brown eyes and a little scar on the back of your right arm between your wrist and elbow." With his long shirt sleeves rolled up, I'd seen that when he lifted his cup to drink. "Oh, and there's a tattoo of an airplane on the back of your left hand. Anything else you want me to remember?" I was puzzled why he'd want me to describe him if the need came for me to testify against him. This wasn't logical!

"Yep," Mike said with a big grin. "That ought tah do it nicely. I hadn't realized you'd observed me so closely. Good that you did. I want you tah write that all down in your notebook. I brought your school stuff in from the van. Your book bag is there on the chair at the end of the table. I added a pen so you could write stuff. I figured you kept your pen in your purse since I didn't see it in the bag." I reached for my thick spiral notebook with its typewriter paper size pages and wrote down his description on a back page. I was still puzzled why he'd want me to do that, but it wasn't wise to question his order. I did as he said to do.

Afterwards, leaning towards him, I said, "Mike, it sounds like I owe you my life. You convinced the person who hired you not to have me killed if I did something for her. What is it that she wants?" I might as well appear to have believed him. I had my doubts about what he'd told me, but his story was leading up to something.

Mike paused and drank some tea. I decided to drink some of mine too. I discovered it had become only warm rather than the hot it was a few minutes earlier.

"Let's come tah that a bit later. First, I want tah introduce you tah the real me. Before I do though, I need your word not tah reveal it tah any police authority." He was frowning. My assurance seemed important to him. I realized that his sense of well-being was important to my own.

It seemed wise not to anger him. I would make a promise that I wasn't sure I'd always keep. Maybe I could get away without giving my word of honor, or even the more sacred one to me, the pledge made as a member of the Unicorn Organization. So, with my right hand raised and my left hand behind my back with fingers crossed, very solemnly I said, "I won't ever reveal what you are about to show me without your expressed and freely given permission." By being so solemn in my presentation of these words, I hoped he would be convinced of my sincerity.

"Okay," Mike said smiling. "I can't stand this any longer. You will be here for some time, so I might as well git comfortable. First off, let me git rid of this long hair that makes my scalp itch." With that, he removed a wig. Underneath was wavy blond hair. Next, the beard came off. Then, Mike leaned over and removed raisers from inside his shoes. When he stood, he looked shorter. He removed the baggy shirt and work pants. Underneath were clean clothes—a blue cotton shirt and denim blue jeans. "Oh, one more thin'," Mike said with a grin. "My eyes aren't really brown." He removed artificial lenses from his eyes. I saw dancing blue ones. I guessed he was watching the amazed look on my face. "Oops, I forgot the scar 'n tattoo. They wash off." I found myself thinking that now I'd seen him as his real person, he might later get rid of me permanently. I was frightened.

We drained the last of the tea from the large cups. I looked at Mike expectedly. Now was the time when he'd tell me what his employer wanted of me. And yet, he stalled. It must be something terribly important and very unpleasant.

Finally, Mike looked at me with a sober expression. "What she wants is goin' tah be hard for you, I know. Remember that I've sworn to make yah dead if'n you don't oblige 'n do exactly what she told me tah have you do. She didn't say so, but I suspect there might be later demands as well. I'm sorry, Cutie, but those are the facts."

"Okay, I understand. What, oh what does she want?" I felt myself trembling.

"Before I tell you more, I need something else. As long as you are my prisoner, you will obey my orders, always tell me the truth, 'n you will never try tah escape from me. Nor will you attempt tah cause me harm now or in the future. You will be on your good behavior. I need your oath on these things." He glared at me. I was afraid. What would happen if I refused making the promises he was demanding? As I debated that question, I realized Mike could easily beat me to death if he got angry enough. He appeared to be about ready to explode as I remained silent. I wasn't sure how long he would keep his temper in check. The longer it took me to reply, the more his face was turning red. He was snapping the joints in his fingers. Mike stood. He gripped my right shoulder with one hand and pulled his other arm back with a fisted hand. Body language told me that I was on the verge of getting hit hard. It was time for me to say something.

"Mike, I can understand what you are thinking, but consider how you worded those requirements. For example, that I would always obey you. If you ordered me to fly to the top of a tree, I couldn't do it—and yet, I'd be breaking my word. Let's change the wording a bit. I agree that if you tell me to do something, and I indicate that I will by saying yes, nodding my head or the like, it means I will obey that order to the best of my ability. That is unless in following your demand, it places me or someone else in serious harm's way. Can you accept this new wording?" I held my breath. I realized we were setting the ground rules for however long I was his prisoner.

Mike paused and then nodded his head. Good, I thought. Otherwise, if I was forced to agree with what he'd asked in the beginning, I would have been his unconditional slave sworn to obey him no matter what he might order. I wondered if he'd get his father's strap to convince me to do whatever was demanded. I could make things easier for myself by appearing to cooperate. "I will never lie to you and also will not attempt to escape. I will never try to do you harm, and I will be on my good behavior while your prisoner. I promise you all these things I've just agreed to," I added with my right hand raised. I was hoping he'd accept my promise, but Mike seemed unsatisfied. The terms he was setting were important to him. He wasn't certain he could trust me. That seemed obvious. He was correct, of course. I'd break this promise if a chance to escape presented itself.

I watched Mike getting more and more agitated. His face was getting red again. He appeared to be trying to control his temper. "I could leave you tied up all the time, or even produce the fatal endin' that would appear tah be an accident," Mike told me. "I think it would be wise for you tah cooperate with me. I'm tryin' tah make things as easy as possible for you, but I need tah be sure you won't double cross me. Remember, I don't need tah keep you alive. My employer would rather have you dead. I'd get a big bonus for makin' sure you were. It's beginnin' tah seem like you're a lot of trouble. It would be easier tah jest forget about keepin' you breathin'. Cin you somehow convince me you'd keep your word if'n I let you live?"

What to do? How to convince him? It seemed important to my well-being that he believed me. I was thinking fast. My life seemed to depend upon being able to convince him I'd keep my word—my parole to him. There was only one way I could think of to do that.

"Mike, in my purse is my membership card in the Unicorn Organization. You've heard, I suppose, than an oath made on a member's word of honor as a Unicorn Organization member is totally binding. If I made such an oath, I'd be locked into keeping it." I sighed. That was totally true. Yet, if I didn't do something, it looked like I could easily end up dead. I'd rather be bound by the oath than that.

"Hmmm," was the only reply from Mike. He got up and left the room by way of the hall door. He returned a moment later holding my wallet. He stopped to look at the two-year old photo of my family taken on my mother's birthday. Then he went on searching through the cards in the special side compartment of the wallet. "I found the membership card," he stated. He closed the wallet and slid it into a back pocket of his jeans. "Yeah, I've heard how sacred a Unicorn member's pledge is. Go ahead, Cutie. Make all you promised bindin'—that is, everythin' you promised me tahday." He looked at me expectantly. I was afraid of the consequences if I refused.

I raised my right hand, formed the Unicorn sign and made the required oath. I had no idea then of the later oaths that would be required of me.

"Okay, NOW will you tell me what your employer requires me to do?" I was getting very anxious about that.

"This will be hard for you, but it has tah be done. You are tah write a letter tah Richard tah break your engagement 'n return his ring. You will not send him any secret phrase or otherwise in any way give him an indication other than you are bein' totally honest 'n sincere in what you write. You cin come up with any excuse you want, but it must sound true 'n realistic. Will you do this? Remember the oath you jest took. Give me an honest answer."

What he asked of me would mean the end of my cherished dream. I moaned.

"Look, Joan," Mike said in a warning tone, "I've sworn an oath as bindin' as your Unicorn one tah see you dead if'n you don't write the letter. I've a big black spider I can irritate 'n git angry enough tah bite you if'n you don't cooperate. I cin tell you have a fear of black spiders. Seems like an appropriate endin' for yah if'n it's necessary. I could then arrange for your body tah be found someplace."

He walked to a corner shelf over the kitchen counter. He removed a jar with a lid and then showed me from across the room the huge black spider contained in the jar. He shook the pint size jar, and the spider moved. Mike unwound the lid and put it in his back pocket. He walked towards me with the jar in his hand. He kept saying things like, "Nice spider" or "Do you bite hard when you're upset?" By then, he was next to me. Suddenly, he shoved my head forward onto the table and pushed the open jar against the back of my bare neck. He moved the jar a little, and I felt the legs of the spider. It gave me a creepy feeling. Mike moved the mouth of the jar across the skin on my neck. It seemed like I could feel the legs of the spider moving. A piercing scream welled up and came out of my mouth. I couldn't stop it. The jar was moved faster, and I thought the spider was getting agitated. I felt like I was going to faint. I screamed again instead.

"Wal, shall I make my pet angry or will you promise tah write the letter?" I reached my hand up to move the jar away. I felt a sharp pain as Mike slapped my hand hard and then shoved it aside. I felt tears in my eyes.

"The spider is gettin' upset," Mike warned me. "It's time for yah tah decide. Which is it tah be---a spider bite or writin' the letter?" He pushed the mouth of the jar harder against my neck.

I was terrified of black spiders. I had a teenage babysitter one afternoon when I was about three years old. She had instilled that lasting fear in me then. "Don't play with black spiders, Joan," she'd said. "They bite and when they do, poison kills. It's a horrible death." She then made all sorts of horrible faces, moaned and shook her body frantically. Finally, she dropped to the floor and played dead. She was warning me to stop teasing a spider in its web with the long pencil I held, but I think she enjoyed playing sort of a game with me. Anyway, she made a lasting impression. It left me with a horror of being even close to a black spider. When she got up laughing, she took a fly swatter from a hook in the kitchen as I watched wide eyed with disbelief. "This is what we do to spiders," she said as she headed towards where the spider had been. For some reason, I was glad the spider had disappeared by then.

No matter what anyone said later about black spiders or how illogical my intense fear of them might be, I had firmly accepted and believed what the babysitter had ingrained in my memory. That was years ago. I needed to face today's problem, and I was really afraid of being bitten by Mike's black spider. I had no doubt about Mike being serious about getting it to bite me if I didn't cooperate.

"Cutie, one last time. Will you write the letter or not?" I couldn't delay the decision.

"Yes," I answered reluctantly. "I will do as you require about the letter. It is better than being dead. Please, oh please, take the spider away!"

Mike replaced the lid on the jar. I saw him smiling when he took the spider with him as he left the room. He returned without the jar and carried a box of stationery instead. I noted he was wearing gloves. The pen with which I'd written Mike's disguise description in my notebook was still on the table. I was thinking hard about how to word a convincing lie to my much loved fiancé. If he didn't believe what I wrote, would I end up dead? *Dead* is such a forever sounding word. I'd do the best I could to write a convincing letter. My life seemed to depend upon it. It would be a set of lies, lies, lies!

When I finished my letter, Mike read it and said it didn't seem right. I should try again. Also, I needed to stress more that I was returning the ring enclosed with the letter. So, I tried again. It was the third attempt that Mike accepted. I felt emotionally drained. I was then instructed to write Richard's first name on the front of the stationery envelope and then his full name and address on the outside of a larger brown padded one. Mike said the correspondence would be sent by registered mail that would need to be signed for before delivery. My heart was breaking as I followed instructions. I didn't like the idea of being dead if I failed to obey orders. I didn't understand the reason for any of this. Seeking ransom from Richard or the Seymours would have seemed more logical.

When Mike demanded the ring, my breathing became shallow. I removed the ring slowly from where it belonged on my finger. I felt a sharp pain and then what felt like a frozen spot deep inside my heart. Trying to hold onto the ring as long as possible, I folded my fingers over it. Reluctantly, I opened my hand when Mike reached for the ring. He was smiling broadly while tears streaked down my face. It was then I wondered if my usefulness to him was at an end. Would I have that fatal "accident" soon now?

A little bit later, Mike was still smiling when he said, "Wal, let's have a bite tah eat before I go tah town tah mail your letter tah my helper. He'll mail it tah Richard from your home post office. You did good with the letter." He started to heat water in the teakettle. "You cin put the cookies on the table," he said handing a package of them to me along with a plate. I noticed he was adding powdered chocolate mix to the cups as I turned. "This'll be ready in a minute. Do you need anythin' while I'm in town? Like, hmm, maybe a box with some girl things? I don't know how long you are goin' tah be here. Maybe you should check tah see if'n my sisters left anythin' like that in the bathroom. If not, I'll buy a box. Go ahead 'n check now while the water is gettin' hot."

I checked in the bathroom corner cupboard and under the sink. I found soap, bubble bath, shampoo, towels and wash cloths, spare toilet tissue, a tube of toothpaste, a package of new toothbrushes and even a new box of what he'd asked me about. I returned to the main room and sat down at the table in my usual chair. "The bathroom is supplied with everything I can foresee I might need for awhile," I told Mike. There was a cup of hot chocolate on the table in front of me. It was in a pretty cup with a daisy design on it. I noticed Mike had his hot drink in a plain cup. I liked mine better.

"Do you like the special cookies?" Mike asked now seated in his chair while watching me closely. I did. They were oatmeal cookies with raisins and nuts in them. The chocolate drink seemed to have a strong flavor. I decided that the mix was probably old. Mike talked with me as we both drained our cups and ate all the cookies on the plate placed in the center of the table. "Maybe I cin pick up some paperback books for us tah read while I'm in town," Mike said after a brief silence. "What kind do you like?" I had the impression that he was working hard to make conversation while under some stress.

I yawned. I wasn't surprised I felt sleepy. I hadn't slept much the night before. And then, I couldn't seem to keep my eyes open. Suddenly, I knew the truth. Mike had drugged my chocolate drink. He wasn't comfortable leaving me alone unsupervised while he was gone. Mike had been watching me carefully. "Maybe you should take a nap, Cutie. I'll help yah tah your bed." He lifted me in his arms and carried me to the bedroom. Holding me up by his right arm, he used his other arm to move the top sheet and blankets off to one side of the bunk. He laid me down with my head on the pillow. I was getting SO sleepy. I could no longer concentrate on what he was doing. In a vague way, I felt my shoes being removed. That's the last thing I knew before I fell into a deep sleep.

I have no idea how long I slept. When I did awake, my head felt fuzzy. A sheet and blanket covered me. I noticed my right foot seemed stuck. I couldn't move it more than a few inches. I moaned and went back to sleep. When I was again conscious, I felt Mike doing something with my right foot. I kept my eyes shut, but I sensed he was taking something away from the ankle. I realized then that he'd somehow secured me to the bed by way of that foot. I sensed him leaving the room. Only then, did I open my eyes. It was dark in the room.

I found myself thinking of the awful letter I'd written to Richard. Dear sweet Richie. I rubbed my finger where his ring had been. My hand felt naked without it. Oh, what would he think when he read the letter and the awful things I'd said in it? Would he believe that I thought he was a spoiled rich boy with whom I would find life miserable while trying to fit into the style his mother would insist upon? I said I knew he was a Mama's boy and that she had a whole lot of influence over him. He'd give in to her demands, like where to live, and it wouldn't be a comfortable simple house like I'd prefer. I added that my wants wouldn't be as important to him as his mother's opinion. She'd probably insist that it was my social obligation as a member of her family to do this or that. She'd likely say a nanny should be hired to take care of our children when I wanted to raise them in the way that suited me.

Thinking about what I'd written in the letter, I realized Mrs. Seymour did not like me, and she would try to mold me to her wishes if I married her son. She'd do her best to control Richard. I'd been a bit concerned about that, but had pushed those thoughts aside. I was hoping these things would work out as Richard and I developed an even closer relationship. I thought about the other accusations I'd made in the letter. I didn't really believe those awful things. Could Richard ever forgive me? Would he want to? Would he give me a chance to explain later? I hugged myself and moaned. Then my eyes closed, and I felt myself falling asleep again. What did Mike put in my drink? How long was the drug going to affect me? Anyway, this time when sleep came, I had a beautiful dream with Richard holding me in his arms while telling me how much he loved me. I was saying I loved him too. I was very happy in the dream, and I didn't want to wake up. I sighed when my eyes opened.

3

Mike's shaking my shoulders awakened me. "What's the matter?" I asked sleepily.

"You've been asleep an awfully long time, Joan. I needed tah make sure you are all right. How do yah feel?" He was looking at me searchingly. "I was afraid you'd died or something, so I decided tah come check."

"Well, I've got a headache for some reason. It should go away when I get up. What time is it?" I felt groggy.

"It's eleven o'clock Thursday mornin'. You've been asleep for about twenty-four hours. I wondered if'n you were still alive." He helped me sit up. I was still dressed from yesterday. He put my shoes on for me while I sat on the edge of the bed. "See if'n you cin stand by yourself without bein' dizzy. If so, best go tah the bathroom 'n splash cold water on your face. I'll wait for you in the other room. Sorry I don't have any aspirin or pain killers tah help with your headache. Lean on me 'n I'll help you up." With his help, I got up carefully, and this time I didn't bump my head on the upper bunk bed. I stood cautiously and felt dizzy for a moment. It passed, and I told Mike I was okay. I'd see him in the main room shortly.

I washed my face and ran my fingers through my hair. I started feeling better. Mike deserved to worry about me, I thought. How much sleeping powder had he put in my hot chocolate yesterday?

When I sat down at the table, Mike had cereal waiting in a bowl for me beside a bottle of milk. He asked if I'd rather have a cup of hot chocolate or tea. When I said tea, he handed me a tea bag and a cup of hot water. We were both silent for a few minutes. My headache seemed to lessen as I ate. Mike continued to study my face. "Your complexion looks better now," he observed. "I think you're goin' tah be okay. I was really worried about you."

I didn't dare say so, but I thought he deserved to worry. If he had to give me the sleeping powder in yesterday's chocolate drink, had he stopped to read the directions? I didn't mention that I knew I'd been drugged. After a period of silence, Mike surprised me by saying he felt we should have code words to identify ourselves to each other in case it should ever be necessary. I wondered about the reason for that.

"I think we should refer tah my employer in this case as Black Crow. I'll be Meadow Lark. I have a helper 'n he suggested we could refer to him as Blue Jay. What name do you choose for yourself, Cutie? Choose somethin' with two words."

I hesitated and then said what I was thinking, "At the moment, I feel like a little brown sparrow caught in a trap."

Mike looked at me sideways, but agreed, "Okay, Brown Sparrow it is."

"Are you expecting trouble? Did something happen while you were in town yesterday?"

"I phoned Blue Jay 'n he suggested that if'n I wanted tah talk tah you about him, a code word would be best. Or, should the need arise, he could identify himself tah you. One thin' led tah another, 'n we decided even my employer should have a code name. So, you have four code names tah remember."

I thought a moment. "Okay, if someone says to me something like, 'Hello Brown Sparrow, I'm Blue Jay,' I'll know he is working with you."

"Yep, 'n you are tah extend your parole tah him automatically. This is tah be as bindin' as the one you pledged tah me. But, my orders will always override any he might give you." Mike looked troubled. I could tell my answer meant a lot to him, but I didn't know why.

"Are you expecting problems? Did you learn something from Blue Jay that troubles you?" I thought I had neatly sidestepped agreeing to Mike's new addition to what I'd promised earlier.

"He said Richard came tah see you Tuesday night 'n was very upset that you weren't there. He felt somethin' was terribly wrong. He said if'n you didn't call or somethin' by tahmorrow that he would file a missin' person's report with the police. He questioned Blue Jay about what he was doin' there. Blue Jay said it would've been a lot easier if'n he had a note from you sayin' what he was hired tah do, or somethin' tah show he wasn't trespassin'. I thought I had everythin' figured out. I hadn't expected a problem for Blue Jay."

I was happy that Richard cared so much. Trying to seem calm, I asked. "So what do you want me to do—write a note for Blue Jay? When will Richard receive my letter? That should take care of the issue where he's concerned."

"I sent your letter by overnight mail tah Blue Jay yesterday. He'll mail it from your local post office via overnight registered mail. Richard ought tah git it maybe by tahmorrow, by Saturday for sure. Once he gits it, he ought tah accept your absence with what Blue Jay told him about your goin' away 'n hirin' him tah take care of your cat 'n things. Blue Jay is afraid if'n anythin' goes wrong, he'll be found guilty of bein' a partner in the kidnappin' plot, 'n we all know what the penalty for that would be." Mike sighed.

I felt indignant. "Well, didn't either of you think about the penalty before you set out on this—this—saving a damsel in distress adventure?" I calmed down and added, "But I do thank you for your efforts. How can I help? Should I phone my next door neighbor, Mrs. Connor? Richard most likely will be talking to her. I could tell her that I've broken my engagement, and I'm going out of town for a few days to avoid Richard. Would that work?"

Privately, I wondered if it was wise to cooperate too much and ease questions about my absence from home. Yet, if too many questions came up, would my body be found someplace? That would account in final terms for why I was gone. Of course, my death would appear to have been an accident. Yes, if what Mike had told me earlier was true, it would be best to keep Black Crow happy. I didn't want her feeling uneasy. I was afraid to gamble on whether or not Mike had been truthful with me about her.

Mike thought a bit before he replied. "Yeah, phonin' your neighbor sounds like good idea. Cin I trust you not tah foul up while makin' the call? Not tah somehow alert her tah feelin' you aren't bein' truthful in what you tell her? Remember your oath!" I simply nodded my head.

"Okay, but make the call short in case the police are on the case this soon 'n decide tah trace calls goin' tah her number thinkin' you might call her—or maybe someone demandin' ransom from Richard 'n usin' her number instead of the Seymour number that would likely be monitored." Mike started smiling.

"You cin do it now, Cutie. 'N you'd better keep your oath or else!" He didn't need to add what the *or else* meant.

I went to the hall phone, and Mike followed me. He stood close enough so he could hear what Mrs. Connor said. "It's a long distance call, so remember tah use a one before dialin' the number." I nodded my head and dialed the number I knew by heart. The telephone rang four times before Mrs. Connor answered breathlessly.

"Hi, Mrs. Connor," I said. She knew my voice so no need to say who was calling. "I hope you haven't been worried about me. I didn't have time to come and tell you goodbye before I left with a friend from college. She was leaving right away and asked me to go with her to her grandpa's funeral several states away. She said she'd pay all of my expenses. She'd never traveled so far by herself and was afraid to go alone. She hopes to stay a few days after the funeral to help her grandma. I'd just broken my engagement to Richard and felt I needed to get away. So, I said yes. We were leaving immediately. Somehow, she got last minute reservations for me. I didn't even have time to pack. I gave my keys to a fellow at college who I know will take care of my cat and stuff. I don't know how long I'll be gone, but I want to let you know I'm okay."

"Oh, Joan," said Mrs. Connor. "I have been concerned. Your boyfriend came by really upset about your not being home when you had a date. I—"

That's when I interrupted. "I'm sorry, but my girl friend just motioned to me that the funeral is about to start. I gotta go. I'll talk with you later. 'Bye." Then I replaced the telephone receiver on its hook.

I was surprised to see perspiration on Mike's forehead. "Did I do okay?" I asked. Mike gave me a big hug. He pulled away suddenly. "Sorry. I didn't mean tah do that, but you did real good. I'm glad I let you make the call. Guess I should call Blue Jay, so he won't worry so much." I nodded my head and went to my room where I shut the door. I took my book bag, my spiral binding notebook and the pen with me.

I was pleased that I had avoided promising to give Blue Jay my parole if in his custody. I suspected the subject would come up again—more ground rules. I went into the bathroom and brushed my teeth with a new toothbrush from the drawer. I was happy to discover that the faucet in the sink now produced water. Mike must have taken care of the problem somehow. I'd seen it before, but again I noticed over the bathtub the attachment that would let me take a shower. I'd take advantage of it with pleasure soon. I went back into the bedroom where I sat on the bed. I wrote in my notebook the code words I'd learned that day. I added what each word represented in shorthand. If someone were to find the notebook, what would look like scribbling to most people would make my notes more secure. (I'd taken two years of shorthand in high school as well as typing and bookkeeping.)

I started thinking more about my situation. I felt I was in danger from Black Crow if someone got too worried about my absence from home and notified the police I was missing. Did Richard still have my Aunt Sarah's telephone number? I remembered I'd given it to him one weekend when I was going to visit her. Would he try to contact her? I'd called her late on the night Richard had given me the engagement ring. I was too excited to wait until morning. Over the years, she and I had formed a close relationship. Since the deaths of my immediate family, Aunt Sarah was my only relative living in this country. I should ask Mike about calling her. She'd get worried if she didn't hear from me soon. She might even make the long drive to come check on me. I generally called her once a week if she didn't call me. She sometimes called two or three times a week. I remembered how excited she was when she heard of my engagement. When she learned I broke it, she'd have plenty of scolding words to say to me. She'd heard of the wealthy Seymours. She told me she'd seen pictures of the family in newspapers. She said I was one very, very lucky girl to be engaged to the only surviving child of extremely rich parents. That impressed Aunt Sarah. She thought married to Richard, I'd end up wealthy too.

Mike knocked on the bedroom door. I opened it. He told me Blue Jay thanked him for calling. "Is there anyone else you should call?" He seemed to be accepting my oath that I would be truthful.

"I was thinking about that. I should phone my Aunt Sarah. She's the only one that matters for a week or so." I thought hard. "I can't think of anyone else I need to phone right away. I started a first aid class with my friend, Susan, about two weeks ago at the Unicorn Organization building. I don't think she'd be upset if I miss the upcoming class. I decided to take the Saturday afternoon class because Richard is busy with his mother on the weekends. I figured that a prospective elementary school teacher like me should learn first aid, and this was a good opportunity to do it. There isn't any homework to speak of, and I could fit it into my schedule. Susan and I meet each other at the class, and then we sit together. I won't need to contact her for awhile because the instructor announced a two week vacation after this upcoming class in honor of the Thanksgiving festivities at the building."

Mike nodded his head and walked with me to the hall telephone. Again, he stood close enough to where he could hear what was said. Aunt Sarah was delighted to receive my call. "Oh, I've been so excited about your engagement," she said. "I've called all the ladies in my lodge. They want to give you a bridal shower. When can you come?"

"Oh, Auntie, that's so sweet of you. But---but---but, I'm not engaged any more. I don't have much time right now to talk about it. A friend from college needed to take a long trip and was afraid to travel alone. She said she'd pay my fare if I'd go with her. I wanted to get away from the house in case Richard came to argue with me. I'm on the trip and have only a minute to talk just now. A fellow I can trust is taking care of my cat and things at home. I want to let you know I'm okay, so you won't worry. I might not call for a few days while I'm on this trip. Besides, if you don't know where I am, if Richard calls to ask, you can truthfully say you don't know. I love you, Auntie. Gotta go…. 'Bye."

"But Joan…" I heard as I hung up the receiver.

"Kind of brisk with her, weren't you?" Mike asked.

"Yes, for two reasons. If her phone was tapped by the police, a short call was best. And secondly, she would have talked for hours scolding me for not staying engaged to the handsome and wealthy Richard. What was I thinking, she'd ask, not holding onto somebody like that? She'd go on and on. I simply just didn't want to hear all of that. I couldn't tell her the real reason." I felt a tear roll down my cheek. Wiping it away, I added, "What seems to impress her most is how wealthy his parents are, and she concluded that Richard would be rich too. His money, or even if it was the lack of it, isn't why I fell in love with him. Still, it's the money and the social position of his family that impresses Aunt Sarah."

Mike nodded, but said, "You seem tah be goin' out of your way tah cover your disappearance. Why?" He seemed to accept that I was helping, but wanted to hear my reason.

"It just seems better to me to keep Black Crow happy at this point. I don't like the idea of a fatal so-called accident in my future. If concerned people make too much fuss, you might get the order to follow through on the alternative plan—my death." I frowned. Again, I was wondering if Mike had told me the truth about Black Crow. Was my life really in danger? I was still afraid to gamble that Mike had lied.

"With what you told Mrs. Conner 'n also your Aunt Sarah, I doubt you need tah write a note for Blue Jay. The plan is all fallin' intah place, but not the way I had it figured." Mike scratched his head. "I know you are wonderin' who Black Crow is, 'n I honestly don't know. She contacted me by telephone. We conducted all of our business that way. Once I had agreed tah do the job, an hour later an oblong package slipped through the mail slot of my office door 'n intah the safety box below. When I checked the contents of the package, I found a fortune in hundred dollar bills. There was a printed note that said, 'Down Payment Only.' It could only have come from Black Crow.

"I'd asked her why it was me she chose for the job. She laughed 'n said she didn't believe I was innocent in last year's legal hearin' that alleged I had checked the brakes of an automobile whose brakes failed five minutes later. The car was involved in a wreck, 'n the driver died. What about my sudden huge bank deposit two days later? She said she felt I'd not given the real reason for that. She didn't believe any of what I'd said while under oath. She was impressed, however, that I was able tah come up with a reasonable sounding alibi. She'd checked 'n found I was known as a person who always kept his word if'n he accepted a job. I sounded exactly like the person she wanted."

Mike looked at me before continuing. "I testified that my lodge friend had complained about his brakes not workin' right. I checked 'n told him he could drive slowly tah the repair garage three blocks away, but it would be far wiser tah have a tow truck take it to the garage. We'd both been shoppin' in the same store 'n met in the store's parkin' lot by accident. He introduced me tah a married couple who were his neighbors. They had also gone tah the store tah take advantage of the huge advertised sales. Their car was parked in the store's parkin' lot two rows over from my friend's car. That's how I'd been identified by name later as the person who had looked at the brakes. I had just finished doin' it 'n was wipin' my dirty hands when his neighbors stopped tah chat a minute. My friend explained that I'd been checkin' his brakes. They didn't stay long enough tah hear me say I didn't have the proper equipment tah do the repair job there nor tah hear me say it was dangerous tah drive that car until the brakes were fixed.

Obviously, my friend wasn't thinking clearly when he approached the intersection just down from the store, saw the yellow signal light 'n pushed down the gas pedal tah beat the red one. I stood watchin' all this from the sidewalk by the store. I wanted tah make sure he made it safely tah the garage. Another driver hit his gas pedal the second his green light flashed. My friend was still in the middle of the intersection. Well, you can guess the rest of what happened. The insurance companies involved were anxious tah pin the blame on somebody who wasn't their client. That's tah be expected, I suppose."

I nodded my head, but didn't offer any remark.

"Black Crow described what I look like 'n the license plate numbers on the two vehicles I own. She told me she even knew I'm engaged tah my secretary 'n that Natalie could be used as an insurance policy tah make sure I'd do what I said I would if'n I accepted the job. Black Crow gave me the creeps. She isn't someone I'd want tah cross 'n have angry with me. The fee she offered was huge. My eyes probably bugged out when she told me the amount. Well, why shouldn't I take the job after she agreed that the fatal so-called accident didn't need tah take place IF'N you'd do what she demanded? The money she offered was lurin' me strongly. She added that if'n I didn't take the job, she'd find someone else who would. I thought the next person she approached would be tempted tah accept the even higher reward for the fatal 'accident' than I accepted for jest gettin' you, Joan, tah agree tah do what she wanted. Black Crow said if'n I changed my mind, the higher fee would be waitin' for me upon proof of your death."

Mike looked at me to see how I was reacting to his story. I didn't say anything, but gave him an encouraging nod to continue.

"I thought it over," Mike went on. "All that money for gettin' yah off by yourself tah do somethin' she required. If'n you cooperated, she'd promised you'd be allowed tah live. SURE, I took the job. I'd get all that money 'n save your life at the same time. What was wrong with that?"

I was thinking out loud when I said, "She sounds like a wealthy person to have been able to find out so much about your personal life and send you the huge down payment. I wonder if it could be Mrs. Seymour? She doesn't want me to marry Richard. She'd be upset when she learned Richard had given me his maternal grandmother's ring. Mrs. Seymour has gone out of her way to embarrass me. I think she has her heart set on Richard marrying the daughter of her special friend, Mrs. Phillips. The daughter, Claudia, and Richard were going steady for awhile before he got interested in me. Who knows, maybe Claudia is Black Crow. I wonder if she would have the available funds for all that has been involved so far?"

"It really doesn't matter who Black Crow is," Mike said. "Facts are facts. I've sworn tah do jest as I told you I would for whatever her reasons are. 'N the sooner Richard gits your letter, the better all the way 'round. Black Crow will probably call my secretary after that with more instructions regardin' you. Until then, we'll jest have tah wait."

4

As Thursday progressed, Mike and I had some long conversations. He said he was thinking of telling Natalie about my kidnapping. He knew he could trust her completely. They had plans to elope over the Christmas holidays. It was only fair to let her know the truth about his current job, he mumbled as if trying to convince himself, but added he was concerned about making her an accessory to the kidnapping crime. Maybe he'd continue letting her think he was guarding a special expensive package until he was told where to deliver it. She might think there was something shady about that, but that was better than creating possible legal problems for her later. Yes, Mike decided while thinking aloud, he'd keep her in the dark about the job that he was currently hired to do. It was important that she act naturally, so he wouldn't tell her about the threat from Black Crow should he fail to please his employer. Since he was going to be careful to appease Black Crow, Natalie shouldn't be in any danger. No need to worry her unnecessarily. Yes, he added in a decisive voice, he'd keep Natalie safe by not telling her everything.

I told Mike how I'd met Richard. It was about six months ago after the finalizing with the lawyer the last details regarding the death of my parents---like the official transfer of the family home into my name. There were a whole bunch of places for me to sign legal papers. Mr. Williams, the attorney, told me my mother had set up a trust for me years ago with the stipulation that I would become the sole trustee of it when I either married or reached the age of twenty-five, whichever came first. He said Mom's directive within the trust said if she died before I became the trustee, then her sister, Sarah, would become the temporary one. It seemed unimportant, so I didn't bother mentioning to Mike that Mr. Williams said he'd been instructed to give me a big brown envelope when I became the trustee and that I should be sure to let him know when I was eligible. I did tell Mike that during the appointment with Mr. Williams, I had to write checks covering final bills charged to my parents and take care of some details that were quite emotional for me. I was lucky that my parents had named both my brother and me---and after the accident, it turned out being just me---on bank documents in such a way that I had no problem obtaining the funds in their bank accounts. These funds were getting quite low by the time I took care of the bills that seemed to become due suddenly. This day of taking care of final details was tiring. Mr. Williams kept bringing up things I needed to do or to know about. Before the office appointment was finished, I felt like I was dealing with the loss of my family as though it had just happened hours ago.

The whole thing was an immense emotional ordeal for me. I was so upset afterwards that I decided to go for a drive. I drove my "Ladybug" car distractedly. I didn't know where I was going or when I'd turn back. I took one road and then turned off someplace else. I drove and drove. I didn't care where I went nor did I pay any attention to where I was at any given time. I was in an emotional turmoil and was using the gas pedal as a release. Not a good idea, but I speeded as much as the roads would allow. After a bit, I had to slow down. The road was steeper and there were more curves. I needed to pay more attention to what I was doing. Gradually, my inner tension eased. Then I was faced with a different kind of problem. My car's engine stopped, and I couldn't get it started again.

I looked at the gas gauge---finally. It said EMPTY. *Oh my, I'm in trouble now.* I looked around. I was on a lonely road in a hilly country. (There were no cell phones or GPS to use in cars then.) What was I going to do? I had no idea where I'd ended up or where the nearest gas station was. There were no passing vehicles in sight. The sun was going to set in about a half hour. I couldn't see any houses or other building. I was lost—completely LOST!

Concentrating on trying to remember what Dad had said to do in an emergency, I remembered to raise the hood of the car. That would signal to a passing vehicle that I needed help. Twenty minutes went by according to my watch, and not a single vehicle came from either direction.

Finally fatigue, the emotional trauma of the day and the past few months, being thirsty and hungry with no water or food in sight—and realizing how foolish I'd been to drive so far and in the manner I'd done it—well, it all caught up to me at once. I found myself with my head over my arms on the steering wheel and sobbing hard. I wasn't aware that a car had pulled in behind mine. I was startled when a man's voice asked me what was wrong. I looked up and saw Richard.

He was unlike anyone I'd ever known. His hair was auburn and fashioned into a formal business style haircut. His eyes were looking down at me with deep compassion. Those brown eyes said volumes. He spoke with a cultured accent. His clothes were casual but looked expensive. I turned to look at his car. It was a late model white one. I noticed the tops of red leather seats visible through the windshield.

"Look, miss," he said, "you can't just sit here. The sun is going down, and it'll be dark in minutes. Did your car break down, or what?"

"When I told him my car was out of gas, Richard replied that he could go back the way he'd come. He thought he remembered seeing a service station about five miles back. I didn't recall seeing it, but I really wasn't paying much attention where I drove that day. He said he could get a can of gas and that should start my car. Then, I could drive back to the station and refill the car's tank. He added that it didn't seem safe for me to stay alone in such a lonely place. We pushed my car to the side of the road, I locked it, and I went with him. When we arrived at the station, it was closed. In fact, it appeared it had been vacated for a long time. Richard looked down at me sheepishly. I noticed he was taller than I am. Anyway, he said he was sorry. Maybe he'd better just take me home. He managed to get me to tell him where I lived. He said it wasn't too far from his house, so it wouldn't be a problem to drive me home. My car was safe where it was, he said, since I'd already locked its doors. Well, what was I to do? I let him take me home."

"Let me guess," said Mike. "He didn't take you straight home, did he? Did he pretend his vehicle ran out of gas too, or somethin'?"

"Actually, he did insist we stop at a restaurant and get something to eat. By then, I was noticing more about him. He appeared to be about twenty-six years old. I asked him what he'd been doing in the area where he found me. He replied that he was checking out some investment property for his father. He found obtaining water there difficult and extremely expensive, so he decided to drive around the area in hopes of seeing a better possible location. Since the whole area was mostly unpopulated, he didn't think it would suit what his father was seeking. I asked Richard during a lull in the conversation if he was married. He said no, but his girlfriend was making suggestions about maybe they should. He said her name was Claudia Phillips. I decided she must be beautiful the way he described her. Then he asked if I had a steady boyfriend. When I said no, he said he couldn't understand why---a pretty girl like me."

"'N you felt flattered," Mike added. I nodded my head. "I was also a little embarrassed. I asked him if he had a picture of his girlfriend. He pulled from his wallet a photo of a gorgeous young woman. He said he'd been dating Claudia since this last January after she broke up with her then current boyfriend. Mrs. Martha Phillips, her extremely rich mother, had taken it into her head that the two of them were going to get married. She wanted them to have a big church wedding followed by a huge reception. Richard's mother, Mrs. Serena Seymour, was delighted with the whole concept. Richard said he felt like he was being pushed into something he wasn't quite ready to do. Abruptly, he changed the subject and asked what I wanted to do about my car. I said I really didn't even remember where I'd left it. I didn't know what I was going to do. He looked at me and shook his head." I smiled at the memory. "He suggested I let him have it towed to my house. He said he knew exactly where the car was."

Mike nodded his head.

"Well, it seemed the simplest way around my problem. I agreed, but only if he'd let me pay him back when he got the bill. He looked at me with a strange expression, but agreed to do that. In fact, he'd been looking at me a lot. He seemed to be studying me and forming an opinion."

"So, how did it happen that you ended up engaged tah him?"

"Well, he did have my car towed to my house. He'd written my address down when he took me there. He refused to come in when I invited him for a cup of coffee that first night. Later, true to his promise, he did come to tell me how much the bill was for having my car delivered along with a can of gasoline. He said his towing insurance paid for it, but he knew I'd fret if I thought I owed him for the bill. He came back two or three times later. He said he was in the neighborhood and decided to check to see how I was doing. One time he suggested I join him for dinner at a certain restaurant. Later, he started asking me out on dates. He said it was just to show Claudia and both of their mothers that he wasn't a pawn for them to move as they saw fit. He said this with a lot of deep feeling. He resented their interference in his life. He said if I didn't have a particular boyfriend, he didn't think I'd mind spending some time with him going special places. Maybe I'd like the outings, but I must understand it was only a way of marking time. He didn't want me to think of him as a boyfriend. He was still interested in Claudia, but wanted their association on his terms. That is, to let things move naturally and not be shoved into something he wasn't ready to accept. Maybe he would later. He cared a lot about Claudia. I was just a way to show he wasn't ready to get engaged. 'Let them get that through their heads!' he'd added sternly. He said he'd be sure to mention his outings with me. That would make them sit up and take notice."

"Not very flatterin' tah you, was he?" Mike observed.

"Actually, I thought him a bit conceited at that point," I admitted. "He was right though. I did like going out, and I wasn't dating anyone. It seemed a reasonable idea for me to have some companionship and him to get his point across to Claudia and their two mothers. I hated going alone to a movie or out to dinner. A girl friend wasn't always available to go with me when I wanted to go. Richard asked if I'd mind taking a picture with him to show Claudia, his mother and Mrs. Phillips. That might convince them more than just words that he was his own man---not a puppet in their hands. I asked if Richard expected me to pay my own way when we went places together under these circumstances. I said it would be only fair. He seemed shocked that I'd even consider such a thing. He told me under no circumstance was I to offer to pay for anything when I was with him."

"What happened tah change things?"

Rubbing my forehead, I answered. "I'm not sure when the relationship changed. I found I was looking forward to our dates and seeing him. He told me I wasn't like the girls he knew. I didn't smoke, nor did I expect my escort to buy me expensive drinks. I always chose a soft drink, milk, water or maybe fruit juice unless I asked for coffee or tea. I explained that alcoholic drinks gave me a headache. It wasn't that I objected to what other people drank. I added that smoking made me cough and cough. It wasn't worth doing for me. Richard said I didn't say catty things. I didn't flirt either. He said Claudia liked doing that with other men when she was with him. I could chat about something other than remarks about other women or the next party. Besides all of that, he suspected I was still a virgin. I know I blushed when he said that. It was none of his business! When it came to choosing a wife, men truly appreciate high moral values, he told me. Finding a virgin is like discovering a treasure, he added. Suddenly, I felt he wasn't one himself, and I wished that he was."

"Let me guess, Cutie. He gradually got you intah the mood for more than jest a kiss 'n hug. He finally made motions tah git more familiar with your private parts."

"Well, he did make motions in that direction, but he was gentleman enough to stop when I told him I didn't want to spoil my wedding night. I said I'd let my future husband show me such things. Richard looked at me oddly and said it seemed only natural to at least make a pass. I smiled sweetly at him and replied that if he wanted to continue being my friend, he'd honor my wishes in this regard."

"'N that's when he asked you tah marry him!" Mike said triumphantly.

"Oh, no! It was three weeks later."

"'N you said yes," Mike added.

"No, I didn't---not then. I told him I wasn't in love with him, but I would like to get to know him better. He agreed to that, so he started dating me once a week. That's all I thought I could fit into my schedule. I was carrying a heavy class load at college, and I wanted to keep my grades up. He said he'd be happy to be with me whenever was best for me. His mother usually had some social thing she wanted him to attend on the weekends anyway. It worked out that Richard and I usually met on Tuesday evenings. By then, it was towards the end of September."

"Your date limitations didn't seem tah discourage him, I gather. He kept comin' back. When did you decide you were in love with him?"

As we chatted, Mike and I each had a bowl of peanuts on our laps. We were sitting on the main room's sofa.

"Oh, it took a bit longer. He insisted that I meet his parents. Seems his father isn't home very much. His mother seemed like a sophisticated snob.

Richard claims she expects his eventual bride would need to be someone who fits into her social set. Richard said that it was his life, and he'd pick his own wife. Furthermore, Mrs. Seymour felt that Richard and his future wife should live in the fancy wing to the Seymour mansion and be available for social engagements in the big Seymour entertainment rooms. Parties and dances are held there often. Pictures in local newspapers and sometimes in national ones of the events are not out of the ordinary. There was a special magazine article with pictures of the mansion and a personal interview including colored pictures of Mrs. Seymour. I noticed that issue of the magazine was on an end table just inside the main impressive door to the Seymour home when Richard took me there. I decided after meeting his mother that she's quite a society lady. The publicity seems to be what she feeds on---important to her own self image."

I gave Mike a sidelong look. "Richard said he'd stopped even thinking of Claudia as a future wife. He discovered he wasn't even remotely in love with her. He added that he counted the days until our single weekly date. He showered me with candy and flowers as well as expensive jewelry. He gave me special attention wherever we went. Yes, I found myself falling in love with him. Not because of all his lovely gifts. No, it was because I didn't feel lonely while I was with him. I didn't cry myself to sleep anymore. I was surprised I could feel so happy. Yes, I realized, I was falling in love with Richard."

"So, it all turned out well for you," Mike sighed. "Like Cinderella 'n the prince." He grabbed another handful of peanuts.

"That's exactly how I felt! How could anyone as wonderful as Richard fall in love with me? I couldn't believe it!

"When he took me to my first party at the Seymour mansion where his mother was the beaming hostess to everyone but me, I felt odd. I felt out of place when my long gown looked like a high school prom formal next to the elegant gowns the other women were wearing. My fingernails didn't have the manicured appearance of the other women's either. And when I tried to carry on a conversation, I found I didn't know anything about the current art exhibit, or the ocean cruise several people were talking about, or even the current events of high society that were subjects of other conversations. People walked around with long stem glasses in their hands. What frightened me most, though, was the change I noticed in Richard. He didn't seem like the same person I knew. Instead of his heartfelt laughs, his smiles, his sharing of inner thoughts, and his complete sense of freedom with me, I saw him become his mother's errand boy. He nodded to various people in a curt manner, acted aloof and seldom smiled."

Mike grinned. "'N his mama didn't like you. Sounds like she was makin' that quite clear."

I went to the kitchen faucet and filled a glass of water. My throat felt dry. I looked sharply at Mike after I took a drink and returned to the sofa. "You're right. Mrs. Seymour didn't like me one bit. Neither did Claudia or Mrs. Phillips. They looked daggers at me. Oh, they were polite enough, but in such a cold way." I bit my lip as I remembered how miserable I'd felt. "I suspect the guests took the pointed rejection of Mrs. Seymour and Mrs. Phillips as their clue, and they treated me coldly as a result. It was all so subtle, yet effective."

"So, you decided you aren't a society gal. What happened next? Did you tell Richard how you felt?" Mike reached again for peanuts.

"Yeah, and he just laughed at me." I still felt angry about that. "He said I'd get used to the swing of things after attending a few more of the social events 'n people would start to accept me. He added that he could ask Claudia to help me select the correct clothes. Price, he said, would be no object. I was upset he'd even think to ask for help from his ex-girlfriend. She obviously hated me. How insensitive was he?"

Mike seemed to think all of this was funny. I glared at him. "Well, what about Richard's father? Did you like him?"

I smiled broadly. "Oh, Mr. Byron Seymour is great! He's so understanding. He said I was the best thing that ever happened to Richard. Said he hoped to see us married, but suggested we make it soon. Elope, he said."

"Am I right in thinkin' that Mrs. Seymour does most of the talkin' 'n decision makin' in their home 'n that, generally, her husband lets her have her way?"

"Yes, I did get that impression, but getting back to my first experience at a Seymour party. Music from a live band started and couples began dancing. I was waiting for Richard to escort me to the dance floor and hold me in his arms. Mrs. Seymour came and grabbed Richard's arm. Looking at me, she said pointedly that she wanted a private conversation with her son. She pulled him away. I stayed talking with a couple Richard had just introduced me to. They soon excused themselves to start dancing. From where I was left standing alone, I could see his mother was keeping Richard in what appeared to be almost a one-sided conversation about something she felt strongly about. I was too far away to be able to hear what was being said. Richard kept glancing at me but stayed next to his mother and Mrs. Phillips. I cringed when Richard walked away from me and headed towards Claudia with a pasted grin on his face."

I shrugged at the memory. It still was hard to forget how terrible I'd felt.

"Deliberately, I moved behind a tall green plant that decorated the corner of the room. I didn't want anyone to see me. From my new position, I was not far from Mrs. Phillips. I overheard her saying to Mrs. Seymour that as his mother, she shouldn't have had to demand Richard go to ask Claudia for a dance in hopes they could talk privately. It would make things easier for the poor dear who was suffering from a broken heart. I remember that when she was with Mrs. Phillips, Richard's mother was the quiet one. Mrs. Phillips would talk on and on. Once Mrs. Seymour asked her, 'Can that really be true? Hard to accept that it is.' And Mrs. Phillips bristled and replied with her distinctive lisping voice, 'It's true. I swear on the memory of my mother.' I wondered what kind of a guarantee that would be, but apparently Mrs. Seymour believed it was a sacred thing to Mrs. Phillips. Richard's mother said, 'Well, I guess I'll have to believe it then.' They had no idea that I was eavesdropping." I sighed as I thought about my unhappy feelings as I stood there.

"I was thinking about finding a telephone to call a taxi when I saw Richard through the foliage as he headed towards where he had left me. I decided to stand out in full view where he could see me. He was coming back finally after dancing six dances with Claudia. Needless to say, I felt disappointed and a bit angry that he spent so much time with her and left me standing all by myself. About then, I overheard Mrs. Phillips with her distinctive nervous laugh. It reminded me of the neighing of a horse. Truthfully, I don't like either Mrs. Seymour or her friend."

I grabbed a big handful of peanuts. My bowl was then empty. "Richard said he and Claudia had a lot to talk about. He was telling her that he and I were going to be married even if I hadn't said yes yet. He didn't want Claudia to be too surprised when it happened. She was arguing that I was a nobody. What was he thinking? He needed a bride with an understanding of how to act with his peers and have at least some degree of social polish. Richard figured she was just jealous. He finally gave up trying to make her understand that he and I loved each other, and that was the most important thing." I sighed. "After that conversation, I asked him to take me home. He said he felt the same way. It was a miserable night. On the way to my house, we stopped and each had a milkshake at my favorite little restaurant. He knew I liked them. It did help settle my upset stomach."

Mike and I spent Thursday getting more acquainted with each other. I discovered Mike's favorite day-off activity was to go out to his boat with Natalie and a picnic lunch. He told me some about her as well.

The telephone rang after we had eaten supper. It turned out to be Blue Jay letting Mike know my letter to Richard had been received and forwarded on. Blue Jay also said my cat was fine and so were my house plants that he'd watered. Mrs. Connor came out and talked with him when he picked up my mail. All seemed smoothed down as far as she was concerned. She wasn't worried about a stranger being in my house now. All this, Mike told me later. He hung up the phone, but stood standing beside it. I knew he was about ready to call Natalie by the soft expression that had come over his face. I smiled and interrupted his thoughts. I said if he didn't mind, I'd tell him good night and then see him in the morning. He nodded and said he hoped I'd have a good sleep. I closed the bedroom door and got ready for bed. After getting comfortably settled under the bunk blankets, I read a few more chapters in my paperback book before turning off the light and going to sleep

5

Friday morning when I awoke, I realized something was different. It took me a moment to analyze what it was. I was hearing rain drops falling on the roof. I noticed the room felt chilled. I dressed hastily. While in the bathroom, I looked out of the window at the back yard. *Is that a rabbit I see? Yes it is!* I watched as it hopped across the yard and then wiggled under a stack of cut wood beside a shed. Then I looked and found a comb in a drawer. I washed it before using it on my curly hair. (Curly hair can be harder to comb than straight hair.) When I felt ready to face another day, I opened the unlocked bedroom door and called asking Mike if it was all right to go into the main room. He said yes, so I joined him there. I wondered what this Friday would bring.

After breakfast, we played checkers for awhile. Mike had added wood to the fire in the fireplace, and the room felt cozy warm. There was newly cut wood stacked in the wood box between the fireplace and the outside door on the west wall. I noticed new newspapers and kindling in the wood box too. Towards noon, Mike said he should go out to the van to listen to the radio. He told me that the radio he had in his room had quit working. He added that there was no television reception at our remote cabin location. Mike looked worried when he returned to the cabin. He said, "The weather report calls for snow here by tahnight."

"Is that a problem? Seems like snow'd be pretty."

Mike was frowning. "We're so far from town that if'n the telephone 'n electric lines git weighed down with the extra snow clingin' tah them, sometimes they break. More often though, it's the nearby things that fall on 'em, like a tree limb with the weight of the snow or where the snow melts 'n the weather turns cold again causin' ice tah form. It could easily take days before the lines would be repaired way out here. This will probably be jest a dustin' of snow though. A bad snowstorm this time of year hasn't happened here in my lifetime. I'd appreciate it if'n you'd please bring in extra wood jest in case the worst happens. I chopped some from the pile of stumps stored behind the shed when I got home from town Wednesday while you were sleepin'. I added that tah the stack of cut wood beside the shed. It won't hurt tah be prepared anyway. We might have tah rely on the fireplace tah heat food. I doubt if the propane company will be able tah fill our tank before the storms hits. When I was in town, I was told their tanker truck was bein' repaired in a nearby garage. It might be next week before it's fixed. The garage had tah send off for a replacement part. A light snowfall doesn't really worry me much, but it would be a good thing tah have extra wood in the house jest in case the weather gits bad. Besides, if'n it rains a lot, the wood on top of the pile would git damp."

Mike had said *please* when he'd requested I go bring in the wood. He wasn't treating me like a prisoner he could order about. And when he asked like he did, I didn't mind accommodating him. He wanted me to stack a lot of wood in the hall.

Luckily, there was a break in the rain, and I was able to keep dry when I went outside. Mike told me there were sheets of cardboard in the shed. He suggested that I could use those to protect the hall wall. As I was placing the cardboard, I noticed Mike was having a serious conversation on the telephone. I didn't stop to eavesdrop. I wanted to get the wood placed inside before the rain started again. A little later, Mike came and helped with the project. I was proud of our accomplishment when I surveyed all we'd stacked in the hall between the outside back door and the one to Mike's bedroom. We'd brought in all the cut wood from beside the shed. Having emergency fuel for the fireplace made me feel more secure. I ignored the splinter that had somehow ended up in my right hand. I didn't mention it to Mike.

I was comfortable sitting on my chair in the main room when the telephone rang. It was late in the afternoon by then. Mike answered the call. "Yeah, that's good," he said. Then his face clouded. "What did you say, Natalie? She wants the writer of the letter tah make a phone call tah confirm receipt of the contents 'n tah repeat with emphasis what the letter said?" I could see Mike, and I could hear plainly what he said. He was getting agitated. "Did she say anythin' else?" A pause, then, "How are you, sweetheart?" Mike turned and closed the hall door. The conversation had become personal.

When Mike returned to the main room, he confirmed the unwelcome news. "Black Crow wants you tah phone Richard 'n ask if'n he got your letter 'n the ring. She says he doesn't want tah believe what the letter said, 'n you are tah phone him tah convince him that you meant every word. In other words, make sure he believes you are refusin' tah marry him. Natalie doesn't know what was in the letter, so she can't guess what the message meant from Black Crow. It's perfectly clear tah me though."

I shook my head in disbelief. Wasn't the letter enough? How could I bear to SAY it to Richard? It was difficult enough to put it into words on paper. With a threatening glare at me, Mike conveyed the penalty for not doing what Black Crow ordered.

"Okay," I said sadly. "I'll do my best. I don't want to end up dead. Shall I do it now? I know his private number by heart."

"Remember your oath, Joan. No tricks—right?" Mike looked at me sternly.

I raised my right hand and made the Unicorn sign. "No tricks, I promise." Soon I heard Richard's voice. My heart melted. "Hello Richie," I said. "I'm calling to make sure you received my letter and that you got your ring back safely."

"Oh, Joannie," said Richard sounding ready to burst into tears. "I've been so worried about you. I'm glad you called."

Mike was standing beside me hearing every word. He nodded to me, indicating I should go on. Remembering the penalty for failing to please Black Crow, I made myself sound as calm as I could. "By now, you should have received my letter breaking our engagement." I had to stop before I could continue. Mike's threatening stare urged me on. "I want to make sure you received the ring. I know it's a family heirloom. You did receive it all right, didn't you?"

"Oh, Joannie. You can't mean you want to call it quits between us. We love each other. I know you love me deeply. You're just getting the bridal jitters. We can work things out. I'll do whatever it takes to make you happy."

My heart was breaking. My voice choked when I replied lying, "Richard, I meant every word of what I said. I refuse to marry you, period. Get that through your head. Did the letter with the ring arrive safely?"

"Why, Joan? What's changed?" It sounded like tears in his voice. "Yes, your letter got here. I read what you said. I just can't believe you're calling quits between us. This is so sudden! I'll put the ring in a safe place, and I promise you that I won't place it on anyone's finger but yours. I love you truly, Joan. Don't do this to us." Richard's voice sounded like he was struggling to keep from crying.

I could hardly say the next words. "It's all in the letter, and I meant what I said in it. Goodbye, Richard." I slammed the telephone receiver back into its hook on the wall. Mike took me in his arms and rocked me gently while I cried bitter tears.

"You did real good," Mike finally said. "Let's hope Black Crow will now be totally satisfied."

"Maybe more words would have convinced him better, Mike, but I just couldn't do it. I love him clear down into the very depths of me. I feel like something is breaking inside after saying all of that to him. He sounded so broken hearted. That phone call was terribly hard to complete without breaking down and crying. What is Black Crow trying to accomplish?"

Mike just shook his head. I decided it was early, but I wanted to be alone. I asked Mike if he minded if I called it a day and went to bed. He looked at me with sympathy. Saying he understood, he said to go ahead. "Leave the door open after you're ready for bed," he added. "That way with the hall and bedroom doors open, the heat from the fireplace will at least take the chill off from your room." I simply nodded my head.

I don't know how much later it was, but with the bedroom door open I could hear plainly what Mike was saying on the phone. "Hi," he said. "It's me, Meadow Lark. Is this a good time tah talk?........Black Crow wasn't satisfied after Richard got the letter. She had Joan call Richard tah totally convince him she was finished with him. Joan did a right good job of it too, but I think she almost had a nervous breakdown afterwards.......... Yeah, but I don't know what else Black Crow will demand next. 'N the radio weather report says it looks like we're in for snow for sure. In the unlikely case that we git snowed in, you still do have the map how tah find this place, don't you?...........Yep, I'll call you each evenin' if'n the phone lines still work. .... Okay, that should work. Thanks, buddy. 'Bye."

I rolled over with my face towards the wall. If Mike checked on me, I wanted to appear asleep. Hours later, I finally was.

■ ■ ■

The next morning, Saturday, it was cold in my room when I awakened. I grabbed the robe and went to the window. It had snowed during the night, and it looked white outside. The sun had come out, and some of the snowflakes glittered like diamonds reflecting the sunlight. Beautiful! I closed the bedroom door and dressed for the day. When I was ready to face Mike, I called out to him from the bedroom door. He said maybe I'd like to make some hot coffee for us. That'd be a nice way to start the day. It was after breakfast when he said I could add wood to the low flames in the fireplace to build a bigger fire so we'd be warm. The thermometer on the porch that I could see from the front window said twenty degrees F. By then, the sun had disappeared behind some clouds.

After the morning routine was done, I decided to do a class assignment from the list Blue Jay had obtained and given to Mike on the telephone. Many of the assignments were pages to read. I took notes as I read. Luckily, I had placed all my textbooks in my book bag that Terrible Tuesday morning. (Book bags for school went out of style when student backpacks became popular.) I had some extra time between classes that day. There were some assignments I expected to complete for two other classes in the study area at the college library.

Late in the afternoon, Mike told me that he thought it would be a good idea for him to go out to the van to check the latest radio weather report. When he came back into the cabin, he was furious. "Some idiots decided tah go for a boat race down the river over by town. There's a county park there with a boat ramp. Well, these two guys had been drinkin' 'n one of them bet the other a hundred dollars he could win a boat race. One thin' led tah another 'n the fools talked their wives intah drivin' their vehicles with the attached boat trailers tah another county park about five miles down the river where there is another boat ramp. Apparently, the boat operators had too much tah drink tah use good judgment. Neither would allow the other boat tah enter alone where the river narrows with the bridge overhead. Goin' down under the bridge abreast, they collided with the double set of bridge supports. They had their boats goin' as fast as possible on full throttle. Both boats ended up with damage, the men were thrown intah the river 'n ended up in the emergency room at the local hospital. A reporter happened tah be there 'n got their full story. It won't be on other than the local news, but I'm glad tah know why the bridge was damaged. Now the highway department has ruled the bridge unsafe 'n has closed it tah traffic. The only route away from here is obstructed by the road over that bridge bein' impassable. We are stuck here until the bridge is repaired. 'N that will take awhile. Stupid, foolish, dumb, irresponsible boat racers!" Mike was upset and concerned about our exit route.

Mike waited until he felt more calm before saying that it seemed like a good idea to get prepared to stay awhile longer in the cabin than he had anticipated. He smiled as he added, "You cin stand on the porch tah take the items I hand yah 'n take them intah the cabin. It'd be good tah git some emergency stuff inside in case we need them."

I put my jacket on and stood on the porch. I noticed the snow was about an inch thick on the ground. There was a stillness in the crisp air. I wondered idly if the rabbit I'd seen earlier was all right. Then I smiled. My older brother, Irving, would have laughed at me and said, "Hey, kid, rabbits are born with a fur coat. Of course, it's warm." I watched as my breath turned into white puffs that looked like smoke. Again, I thought of Irving and how we'd pretended we were smoking cigarettes on a cold day long ago. Nice memories!

After handing me a bag of canned food, Mike went down the porch steps and walked towards the van. He stepped over the mound of snow that clearly showed the location of the tree roots. He made several trips back and forth. I carried the items inside the cabin. Finally, he told me he had only one more trip to make. He added that he had just checked again, and the very latest radio report said that the weather forecast had suddenly changed. We could expect up to three feet of snow in our area. The weather reporter said a snowstorm seemed about to mature into something not seen during November here in forty-two years. I supposed it was good to know what the forecast was, but with us being stuck in the cabin until the bridge was repaired, this latest news wasn't welcome. Well, worded differently, it was good to know what to expect, but what was in the forecast was not pleasing to hear.

I watched as Mike lifted a large oblong container from the back of the van. I saw him set the wooden box down and then make certain all the van windows were rolled up and the doors were all locked. I casually watched Mike start up the path carrying the heavy load. The way he struggled carrying it, I decided the box must weigh at least seventy-five pounds. It seemed awkward to carry for some reason.

Looking beyond Mike, I noticed the especially pretty sunset. Various clouds assumed brilliant colors. It took my breath away.

I heard Mike say, "OOFFH!" I looked. He was stumbling and trying to catch his balance. Obviously, he had tripped on the roots over the path. The way he'd held the box, it would have been difficult to look downwards. As he fell, he lost his hold on the box. Mike landed on his butt with his legs bent at the knees. The sharp corner of the heavy wooden container crashed down on the lower part of his left leg with an ominous snapping sound.

My foot was poised over the top step when I paused. Had I promised not to leave the cabin and the porch? No, I decided. I had not, so I hurried to Mike. I struggled to move the heavy wooden box off to the side. I saw something was wrong. Mike was clutching his injured leg and moaning with pain. Tears were running down his cheeks. With him leaning on my shoulder, we struggled to the porch. He barely made it up the steps when he fainted. Somehow, I managed to drag him inside the cabin and then shut the door. He was too heavy to lift onto the sofa, so I left him on the floor. Knowing the supplies would be needed, I dashed to get the first aid box. It was on the counter beside the refrigerator. By the time I returned to him, Mike was conscious and blinking his eyes.

With Mike's half-hearted help, I managed to get him onto the sofa. During the process, I had my hands under his armpits. Under his left shoulder, I felt a holster underneath his jacket. I felt a little more. Yes, there was a gun fastened inside the holster. He was helpless to stop me from taking it away from him in his weakened condition. I let the moment pass. Regardless of what the truth was, at that moment I wasn't considering him as my kidnapper, but rather as my protector. I felt he would try his best to prevent Black Crow from ordering my death. Still, if she ordered it, and he couldn't persuade her differently, I'd probably end up dead. I knew that, but I wasn't thinking of it just at that moment. Other thoughts buzzed through my mind, but they were interrupted by Mike's deep moan.

I wondered just how badly he was injured. I needed to check his leg. With his permission, I pushed my hand up inside his pant leg. I stopped short when I realized he had a fracture in one of his shin bones. The break was about halfway between his knee and ankle. I hadn't finished my first aid class, but I knew this was a bad thing. He was going to need to have it set. I was no doctor and there wasn't any near. I sighed. I felt a feeling of panic. Grateful for what I'd learned so far in the first aid class, I took a deep breath. Then, as calmly as I could manage, I asked him if I could rip the seam of his pant leg so I could take care of his leg. "Sure, go ahead 'n play nurse," Mike responded while gritting his teeth in pain.

I used the seam ripper from the first aid kit to undo the threads on the outer lower left leg seam of Mike's jeans. Ripping the threads at the seam took a little longer than just cutting the fabric, but the seam could be re-sewed later. At this point, the few extra minutes taken to rip threads instead of cutting fabric didn't seem important. Besides, it gave me a little time to gain my composure. I wished we had some pain killers to give Mike, but there were none in the first aid kit. A little bottle was there for them, but it was empty. Someone had used the pills and hadn't thought to refill the bottle later. Mike said he didn't have any pain pills in the cabin either.

I discovered Mike had a fractured tibia, the largest of the two shin bones. He was lucky that he didn't have a compound fracture. If he'd had one of those, the edge of the broken bone would have punctured his skin. I remembered that much from the first aid class. I realized, however, that Mike would have severe bruising as a result of the heavy box falling on his leg. If it weren't for the broken bone that I needed to set, I would have packed his lower leg with cold snow. He fainted when I jerked his foot to align the bone correctly. Regretfully, I wondered if I should have pulled the foot more slowly and gently. I hadn't gotten far enough in the first aid course to know the proper procedure. While he was unconscious, I worked hurriedly to bind the leg with the bone in place. I used the smoothest pieces of the kindling for splints, and I rolled newspapers tightly over and around them to prevent splinters. I used tape from the first aid kit to wind around the top and bottom of the newspapers to prevent them from unwinding. Then I wound gauze tightly over the splints and around his leg. I used tape to hold it all together and in place. I hoped it would prove to be satisfactory. I'd felt clumsy and inadequate while doing my best, but at least Mike's bone was back in place. I hoped it would stay there.

After he regained consciousness, I wondered if Mike was thinking clearly when he said, "NO!" in a strong tone when I asked about my calling for an ambulance. As I thought about it later, I realized an ambulance couldn't get over the bridge to reach us. Mike said I should call Blue Jay instead. I felt a surge of relief knowing that I would be told how to reach Mike's partner, and then I would not be totally dependent upon Mike. What if he died? Now, I would have the telephone number of someone who knew the location of the cabin.

Mike gave me a forced smile. "Make the phone call," he said. He gave me the number, and I wrote it down on the back of my notebook cover. I had taken the notebook and pen back into the main room so I could take notes about my reading assignments while at the table. The notebook was the closest thing to write upon. "It's a long distance call," Mike told me, "so be sure tah dial a one before the number." I went into the hall and made the call. I wondered what would happen if I didn't reach Blue Jay. Mike must trust him a lot to feel his partner would come to our aid. What if Blue Jay couldn't or wouldn't help us? Would Mike think of a different alternative? All this was going through my mind as I waited for someone to answer the ringing telephone I was calling.

Finally, a woman answered on the sixth ring. I asked to talk with her son like Mike had said to do. When a male voice answered, I said, "This is Brown Sparrow. Who are you?" I was thinking if the wrong person had answered, he'd think it was a crank call and hang up the phone. I had taken it for granted that Mike had told his accomplice the code words.

"Blue Jay," the voice said with a distinctive accent that I didn't recall ever hearing before. I told him Code 800---the code word for help Mike had told me before I dialed the number. When I explained what had happened, Blue Jay replied, "I'll check to see what I can do and call back shortly."

"Let me tell Meadow Lark that," I answered. "Maybe he'll want to add something." Mike shook his head. "He says no," I added.

Blue Jay asked something that surprised me. "Are you all right, Joan? I've been concerned about your circumstances, but I was promised you'd not be molested or hurt. Frightened maybe, but not injured." Blue Jay did sound sincerely concerned.

"The promise has been kept," I stated softly. I'd rather Mike didn't hear this part of the conversation for some reason. Louder, I asked. "Are you aware that we have snow on the ground here?"

"I'll check the weather and road conditions, and then I'll make plans," Blue Jay answered. His voice sounded like he was talking through a sock or something. It seemed muffled. I wondered if he was trying to disguise his voice. "I'll call back within the hour," he promised. Then, he ended the call.

After telling Mike that Blue Jay said he'd call back soon, I put more wood on the fire in the fireplace, set a kettle of water on the stove to make something hot to drink and wondered what was going to happen next. Just then, I became aware that Mike was asking me something. I turned towards him.

"Cutie, I know you felt the gun I'm wearin' when you helped me off the floor. You had your hands under my armpits. Why didn't you take my pistol from me when you had the chance? You know I couldn't have stopped you."

I looked at him steadily and replied, "Well yes, Mike, I did know I could do it, and I did think about it for an instant. I've promised not to try to escape and what else would I need the gun for? Besides, it would not have been the good behavior that I've promised to keep. In no way could I take the gun without violating my sacred oath."

In addition to my other thoughts, I remembered thinking at the time, *Just what would I do with the gun if I had it? I can't force Mike to take me home under the present circumstances. I had a hard enough time getting him into the cabin. Getting him into the van is out of the question. I don't know how to get home myself even if I demand the van keys. If I take a wrong turn or get stuck someplace, I might be stranded for a long time. I could run out of gas too. With the cold weather, getting stranded some place isn't a good prospect. And besides, Mike said the only way out is by the route where the bridge has been damaged. Even if I was free to go---and I'm not---I'd be wiser to choose to stay in the shelter of the cabin.*

And it was true, I had promised not to try to escape as well as to be on my good behavior. Stealing Mike's gun would have violated my oath in a big way. Why was it that my oath was totally unbreakable? Had I somehow been brainwashed into believing that? It seemed like even if my life was at stake, I couldn't break such an oath. Well, I'd think about that later. Now that he questioned me, it was a good idea to keep in Mike's good graces and to give him more reason to trust the worth of my Unicorn Organization member's oath. That might become an important issue later. Besides, something in me had rebelled against thinking of leaving Mike alone when he was in such pain. Maybe too much compassion was a weakness, but I couldn't help what I'd felt. Obviously, there was no choice anyway—the exit road was blocked.

Mike looked at me, then smiled. "I guess I'll never question you keepin' your word again. You've proven tah me several times that it's sacred tah yah. Like, when you stopped on the porch before comin' tah help me. I could plainly see on your face what you were thinkin' 'n when you remembered you had not promised tah stay there. Do you know how tah use a gun? If'n it's necessary, would you know how tah use mine?" He told me the make and model number of it. It was a popular revolver choice among gun owners.

I nodded. "My father taught my brother and me how to handle guns. He said it probably would never be necessary, but we should know how. He even took us target shooting. I got pretty good at hitting what I aimed at." I smiled at the memory. "His favorite gun was his pistol like yours. Yes, I know how to use it. My favorite gun of his was his twenty-two rifle. My brother liked my father's thirty-thirty rifle best. It had too much of a kick for me to enjoy firing it. I always ended up with a bruised shoulder when Dad insisted I practice a little with it from time to time."

I prepared a cup of hot tea for Mike and one for myself. I noticed he was shivering. I remembered from my first aid course that injured people might go into shock. A blanket should be placed over them. I set the cups down on the table and went into my bedroom. I pulled the two blankets and heavy bedspread from the top bunk. I took these into the main room. Then I went back and brought the two pillows from the top bunk plus the top sheet. First, I placed the sheet over Mike, and then I covered him with the two blankets. I suggested that if he got too warm, it would be easy to remove one of the blankets. He ended up covered by the sheet and two blankets while situated on top of the sofa's afghan with two pillows and the folded bedspread supporting his head, shoulders and back. The decorative pillow from the sofa was under his left knee. I hadn't thought ahead to remove the afghan on top the sofa before Mike ended up there.

Nor was I able to move him to lean against the arm of the sofa. I felt if he turned a little on his side, he'd be able to drink from his new position now that his head was elevated a bit with the help of the pillows and the folded bedspread.

He and I were both sipping our tea when the phone rang. Mike nodded to me, and I went to answer it. As we expected, it was Blue Jay. He said he'd checked with the highway department and found that the only road into our location was not passable. A bridge was out. Weather for the next day called for a very heavy snowstorm in our area and in his as well. It would be dangerous trying to reach us until the storm passed. I repeated all that to Mike.

"Tell him that it's likely the phone here will be out of order 'n our electric power will be off if'n the storm is bad. We won't be able tah communicate if'n that happens. We'll have tah rely on his judgment about how tah rescue us," Mike was frowning. "Ask him tah call my secretary 'n tell her that I'd asked him tah call her tah let her know I hope she can meet me at the hospital when he is able tah git me there. Say that our phone service will likely be affected by the incomin' storm 'n she 'n me might not be able tah communicate for a time. Ask Blue Jay tah tell Natalie that he'll keep her posted when tah meet me at the hospital."

I relayed all that to Blue Jay. "Okay, I can do that," he said. "Tell Meadow Lark that I do remember that his secretary doesn't know the facts about his current job, so I won't tell her either. It's a good thing she was told before this that I'm working on this particular case with her employer." Mike said he couldn't think of anything else to convey to Blue Jay. I passed that message on.

"I'll do the best I can," Blue Jay replied. "Hopefully, your phone will stay working. 'Bye."

It was dark outside when Mike asked, "Will you go out 'n bring the box in that we left outside? It'll be heavy, so be careful. If'n it's too heavy for you, come 'n tell me 'n I'll figure some other way tah git the items inside." Mike sighed. "Bringin' the box in turned out tah be a disaster, but we might need the contents."

When I studied the box in the glow of the porch light, I decided to kneel in front of it, angle it up onto my shoulder and then stand while holding the box firmly. I staggered as I tried to get to my feet. Finally, I was standing. That box was HEAVY, and the weight wasn't distributed evenly. I felt whatever was in the box must be important. Mike seemed to feel it was necessary to get the box into the main room of the cabin. I felt victorious when I was successful getting it there.

Setting it down on the floor was tricky, but I did it. Mike said to slide the box under the main room's big west window. Just pushing the box there was a major chore. I felt exhausted! I sat down on the floor and took deep breaths. My shoulder ached where the weight had dug into it. I sincerely hoped whatever was in the box was worth all the trouble it caused. For some unknown reason, I was hesitant to ask Mike about its contents, and he didn't volunteer any information. I felt really disappointed that he didn't, but I reasoned he'd tell me later. I studied the box more carefully. It had a hasp fastened by a stout padlock. That made me more curious about the contents. I imagined it could be all sorts of things, like a shotgun with plenty of ammunition, dynamite, signal flags, animal traps, or some other possible items that crossed my mind. Mike never did tell me what was so important in that box. I guess I'll always have some conjectures about what it could have been.

Memories of what had happened in the last few days were still vivid in my mind that evening. They gave a backdrop to what was happening at the present time. I realized a big change had taken place between Mike and me. He was leaning on me to do necessary things. Our relationship had become almost like partners in an emergency. He was no longer thinking of me simply as his prisoner. I still vividly remembered the fact though. I was relying on him to keep me alive. He had an accomplice willing to help us get away from the cabin, and Mike was trying his best to convince Black Crow to let me keep on living. It seemed wise to help Mike as much as I could to help us both survive.

Somehow, Saturday had slipped by. I stacked extra wood on the fire. I knew with him sleeping near the fireplace that Mike should stay warmer than I would. I remembered seeing a tall bottle of water in the refrigerator. It had a tight lid. I emptied it into the kettle I'd use for making tea later. Then I wound the lid back on. Handing the bottle to Mike, I said, "Maybe this will save you a trip to the bathroom." He acknowledged my thoughtfulness with a brief nod and placed the bottle on the floor beside the sofa.

I kept my clothes and jacket on when I went to bed. I thought it would keep me warmer. I left my bedroom door open and asked Mike to call me if he needed anything. He said he would. I wondered what the next day would bring. I felt a lot of stress as I worried. Sleep didn't come for a long time.

For one thing, I kept wondering which of the women who knew me could be Black Crow. I remembered that Aunt Sarah was the trustee of something until I either reached age twenty-five or married. Was the trust large enough to tempt her to stop my marriage so she'd have access to the funds longer? If so, I thought the threat to order my death was something to create results, but she wouldn't actually order it. I knew she loved me. Perhaps she expected Mike to bargain with her to avoid the so-called fatal accident? Besides, where would she get all the money to do the research about him and then send him the huge down payment for the job? Or did it come from the trust funds? I had never heard of the trust until the attorney told me about its existence. Would Aunt Sarah borrow money to cover paying Mike? Was it just an act about being so happy about my engagement? Would she order Richard's death if she felt it suited her? How would she know so many details—like Richard's reaction to my letter? Well, he had probably called her. Yes, Aunt Sarah might be Black Crow, but somehow I doubted that she was.

I could picture it being Mrs. Seymour or even Mrs. Phillips. I wondered if Claudia cared so much about Richard to want him enough to pay such huge funds. And was there someone else I hadn't thought of yet who would be delighted to see the end of my engagement to Richard? Had a woman wormed her way into Richard's life and wanted him as her husband---or access as his wife to his family's fortune? Maybe Richard had touched the heart of one of the society women at the various gatherings at the Seymour mansion. If so, he seemed unaware of it. Well, I couldn't do anything about Black Crow now. I had come to believe she actually existed. At first, I'd thought Mike was lying about her, and that it was a plot to get the expensive ring while making both Richard and me think it had slipped out of the envelope en route to him.

Then my thoughts turned to Mike and his broken leg. I wondered how to treat the bruises while the splints were in place. I worried about the upcoming snowstorm. It sounded like it was going to be bad. It could adversely affect Mike and me. Could I ask him tomorrow about letting me drive us to town and a different location? No, that wouldn't work. Blue Jay confirmed a bridge was impassable on the only road exit away from the cabin.

If it was going to be up to Blue Jay to rescue us, how could he do it? Maybe we wouldn't be isolated very long. Things often look worse when speculated about than they did when events actually happened. Thinking that, I finally rolled over and went to sleep.

6

Sunday dawned clear and cold. At least it felt cold in my room when I awakened. I realized the fire had probably gotten low in the fireplace. Since I'd slept in my clothes, I was ready to slip into the other room and add wood to the fire. I put my shoes on to help keep my feet warm, and I tiptoed into the main room hoping I could add the needed fuel without waking Mike. When I quietly entered, I found him already awake. I was surprised when only ashes met my eyes in the fireplace.

"Sorry, Mike. I didn't wake up early enough to add more wood to the fire. Guess I'm accustomed to you taking care of details like that. I'm glad you didn't try to get up and add the wood yourself this morning. I haven't had any experience with fireplaces before. BUT---I'll learn." I smiled when I noticed there was fluid in the tall jar I'd left with Mike the night before. I'd empty it shortly in my bathroom. Giving the jar to Mike had been a least one thing I'd done right. I worried about Mike's broken bone, and if it would stay set the way I had situated the splints and tried to keep them in place. Letting the fire go out wasn't a good thing.

"Do you know how tah start a fire in thar?" asked Mike. There was doubt in his voice.

I shook my head and shrugged. "It can't be that hard," I said defensively. "I could put newspapers down, add some kindling, and then on top of that put some bigger chunks of wood. My problem would be finding the matches to light the paper."

Mike laughed. "You make it sound simple. The matches are in the drawer under the sink. The same ones you've been using tah light the burners on the stove. Why don't you see how good a fire maker you are?" He said it like it was a dare, and he didn't believe I'd be successful. He turned out to be right. I laid the paper flat over the cold ashes, piled some kindling in flat rows over the paper, and then added two pieces of bigger wood flat over that. I decided I was ready to light a match to the paper. And while some of the paper burned, the kindling didn't catch fire.

"What did I do wrong?" I asked puzzled.

"Start over. Move the kindlin' 'n the bigger wood off to one side." I did that. "Now, take the sheets of paper 'n crinkle 'em so they make a big glob. You'll need tah add more paper than you started with. We don't have a grate, so place the paper glob down on top of the cold ashes." I did that. "Next, take at about ten or twelve pieces of kindlin' 'n lean them upright against the paper."

I laughed. "You mean make sort of a tepee over the glob of paper. It reminds me of what a child might think of to play with."

"Wal, I hadn't thought of it like that. Next, take three of the larger pieces of wood 'n add those leaning upright on top of the kindlin', but in places where a little of the paper shows from underneath."

When that was done, I asked, "And then what?"

"Now is when you take a lighted match 'n ignite the paper." I followed his instructions and then stood back to watch the results. "'N don't forgit tah pull the screen over the front of the fireplace," Mike added.

I felt victorious when we soon had a warm fire glowing in the fireplace. I checked to make certain the door to the hall was closed to keep the warmth in the main room. I heated water on the stove to use with condensed coffee granules. I looked in the cupboards to see what I should use for breakfast. I ended up placing two bowls filled with dry cereal and a bottle of milk on the table. I added the two big cups we'd used before and two spoons. Once a big spoonful of coffee granules was added to each cup, I poured hot water on top of them. The next problem was to figure out how to bring breakfast to Mike on the sofa. I decided to use a chair as a portable table. I moved one near Mike, turning it so the back was away from the sofa. Then, I placed his breakfast on the seat of the chair. I asked if he would like sugar or anything in his coffee this morning. I knew he usually had preferred it just plain before. He replied black was still fine. I used a little sugar in mine. As I was eating my breakfast, I began to wonder how to make a set of crutches for Mike. I asked for his thoughts about that.

"Wal, when I git tah the hospital, I'll likely be given a set," Mike decided. "In the meantime, you could loan me your shoulder if'n I need tah move. On the other hand, if'n you was tah saw the back of a chair off from its seat 'n its two front legs, I could use that. These chairs have taller backs than most chairs. It ought tah work. You could go git a saw out in the shed. 'N while outside, you could turn off the valve on the pipe leadin' intah the house by the spring. You would need tah fill containers with water first though." Mike paused and then told me where to find the key to the small tool shed. He added that if the weather turned as cold as he was expecting, the water pipe to the cabin would likely freeze and maybe break if the valve wasn't turned off. A broken pipe would create a messy problem when the thaw came, he explained.

"'N when all the water containers are full, 'n the outside valve is turned off, then open up the faucets in the kitchen sink 'n in your bathroom. The pipes need tah be drained. When the water stops flowin' you cin turn the faucets back to the off position. Once I have my makeshift crutch, I can open up the faucets in my bathroom. You are not tah go intah my room or its bathroom."

I filled all the kettles I found in the kitchen. I started filling bowls, cups and glasses. Then I filled the bathtub in my bathroom, so I could use that water to flush the toilet and use for washing. When I'd filled every container I could find, I was ready to cut off the water supply to the cabin. Mike explained exactly where to find the cut-off valve and where the spring was. I donned my jacket. I reached for the gloves usually in its pocket before remembering I'd left them at home before going to college on that Terrible Tuesday which now seemed weeks ago. The weather had looked so nice that day, I didn't think I'd need either my gloves or the wool hat my mother had knitted for me. I'd left both at home, but I wished I had them with me now before going outside. I thought of home, wondered about my cat, and when I'd be able to feel safe there again. I felt a surge of homesickness.

When I came back from doing the outside chores that Mike requested, I removed my shoes in the hall. They were wet from the soft snow. I set them on the brick hearth in front of the fireplace to dry. I placed the saw from the shed there too until I was ready to use it. A bit later when I attempted it, I had trouble getting the saw to cut into the wood of the chair. Maybe that was because I'd never used a large saw before. Anyway, it took time, but Mike had his crutch finally. I wondered if the chair had been part of a set that had been in his family a long time. If so, it was a shame to destroy it. Maybe the parts could be glued back together later. If would have to be mighty super strong glue to work though. Oh well, it wasn't my problem. We discovered that Mike needed a cushion at his armpit when he used the chair crutch. The soft decorative sofa pillow turned out to be perfect for that.

I started to sit down at the table when Mike said, "I've been thinkin'. When Blue Jay comes tah rescue us after the snowstorm, everythin' outside is goin' tah look white. It might help if'n we could have black smoke comin' out of the chimney. 'N the only way I can think of doin' that with what's available tah us would be tah burn a tire in the fireplace. 'N the only spare tire I cin think of is the one from the van. Do you think you're strong enough tah git it 'n brin' it intah the cabin? After all, you're a mite of gal—what, about one hundred 'n ten pounds?" I nodded my head. Actually, I weighed one hundred fifteen pounds, but his estimate was close enough. "Would you like tah try?"

I agreed. I put my shoes back on. I'd discarded my jacket when I'd finally gotten warm after my earlier trip outside, but now it went back on. Somehow, I did manage to bring the spare tire onto the porch. Neither Mike nor I could think of anything else we could do to prepare for what we knew was probably in our near future. I gave the van keys back to Mike while telling him I'd made sure all its windows were closed and the doors locked. Neither of us had even considered that I would drive the van away once I had the keys. Where would I go with the bridge out blocking the only way to leave the area?

Luckily, the electric lights, propane stove and telephone were still working by that evening. Mike asked me to call Blue Jay to find out if there was any news from him and also to tell him about the black smoke that would be coming from our chimney after the predicted snowstorm.

I made the call. A lady answered, and I asked to talk with her son. Blue Jay said in a puzzled voice, "Hello?" We exchanged code words. I relayed Mike's message telling him to expect black smoke from the chimney. I asked if he had any idea when he'd be coming. He replied that the storm was supposed to be over by late Wednesday. From the reports, it seemed even the valley was going to get snow. This storm was definitely being called a freak November one now in the weather reports. It was expected to be worse than the storm in November forty-two years ago. If all goes well, Blue Jay told me with the accent I now associated with him, we could expect him on Thursday, hopefully in the morning. I relayed all of this to Mike.

"Remind him that I'll need help walkin'," Mike asked me to tell Blue Jay.

"Okay, I'll keep that in mind," Blue Jay replied. "The black smoke will help immensely. I'm working on a plan, but everything isn't concrete yet. Ask Meadow Lark if there is a clearing near there."

Mike said there was one about a quarter of a mile down the road to the north of the cabin. I repeated that to Blue Jay. I'd no sooner said that when the telephone went dead. We were lucky to be able to tell Blue Jay as much as we did. "Oh, there isn't any signal. The line is dead!" I told Mike in frightened tones. "What's going to happen now?"

"Hmmmm. Look outside 'n see if'n it's snowin'."

I went to the front door and opened it. What I saw in the glow of the porch light that I turned on was a fierce wind making the trees bend and sway. When I told this to Mike, he shook his head. "We'll be losing electric power soon is my guess. Maybe it'd be a good idea tah heat water while we cin tah make one last drink of hot coffee before it's too late. The propane truck never got here tah refill our tank 'n we can expect the stove tah quit workin' any time now."

While the water was heating, I went into my bedroom. I retrieved my little flashlight from my purse and placed it in my pocket. I was glad Mike gave me back my purse without removing any of its contents the day after I'd after I'd given him my parole. I returned to the main room and put more wood on the fire. By then, the water was hot. I added it over the condensed coffee granules in the two cups and handed one to Mike. He still had the chair-table beside the sofa.

"Wal, seems like I missed a few things in my plans," Mike said trying to sound cheerful. "Guess I made a few mistakes as I didn't reckon on some un-knowns. Still, you don't have tah worry. Blue Jay cares what happens tah us 'n will come tah our rescue. We jest have tah git by until Thursday. Now, when you look at it that way, it isn't so bad, is it?" I wondered if he was just trying to keep my spirits up. Did he really feel that way?

I counted on my fingers while thinking, Sunday night, Monday, Tuesday, Wednesday, and then Thursday. I wondered if we had food for that long. I thought we had enough wood for the fireplace. We had plenty of water, and if worst came to worst, I could bring in snow and melt that to drink. A big concern was having Mike wait that long to get to a doctor. I was beginning to feel Mike was my friend in spite of the circumstances. I worried about his getting a bad infection in his leg and coming down with a high fever. If he died, I didn't know who Black Crow might send to create the fatal so-called accident for me. My welfare was interwoven with Mike's. There was nothing I could do to change things. Best just make the best of it---and be grateful Blue Jay would rescue us when he could. That was a bright ray of hope.

"We'll manage," I told Mike. "I suspect it would make sense for me to move the mattress and bedding from my bunk bed into the main room. It's going to get cold in my room from what looks like is on the way. With the fire going in the fireplace, and me here to be sure it doesn't go out like it did overnight before, we should keep warm. What do you think?"

Mike agreed with me, so after the coffee cups were empty and washed, I dragged my mattress into the main room and went back to get my bedding. I placed the mattress on the floor between the table and the sink. I didn't tell Mike, but I knew Richard would have suggested we sleep together if it were him and me involved---to help keep each other warm, he'd have said. I made my bed and then sat down on a chair at the table and faced Mike.

"Would you like me to hand you one of the books you purchased in town the other day? Might help the time pass," I said. "Think I'll try reading one too."

Reading is exactly what we decided to do until we were ready to go sleep. Luckily, the electricity was still working. A half hour later when I was reading in bed, I heard a slight noise and looked up. Mike's book had slid to the floor. His eyes were closed. I didn't stop reading my exciting mystery story until a bit later. Then, I rolled over towards the sink and soon fell into a deep sleep. I hadn't thought about getting up to turn off the light.

7

The next three days—Monday, Tuesday and Wednesday—somehow passed. I'd taken the time to chop the van's spare tire, and we tried it out to see if indeed it would produce the hoped-for black smoke. Luckily, it did. Our food supply held out. There was ample water for our needs. Our wood was diminishing, but we still had some remaining. The fireplace kept the chill away from us. Out of the front window, I'd watched the snow pile up. The wind blew fiercely at times. I was glad we had a safe haven in which to sit out the storm.

In case the propane tank became empty, and we could no longer use the stove, Mike had figured a way to warm food inside the fireplace by placing the corners of an oven rack over four of our empty cans weighed down with small rocks. I'd need to wait until the fire left only hot coals before I tried cooking there, Mike warned me. He said to find the tallest cans in the garbage bin. I should then remove the labels and wash the cans. Make sure, he added, that the four cans I chose were all the same height. After that, I should get stones to help weigh down the cans so they wouldn't tip over. I found the small rocks beneath the snow by the back step where Mike said he'd stacked them months ago. Mike said he was hoping they'd come in handy some day---and besides, he added, they were pretty. I discovered there were several different types of small stones in the pile. I'd never noticed before that each rock has its own personality. Mike said if they weren't covered by snow where we couldn't see them, larger rocks would be better than the cans for our purpose, but we'd need to use what we had. He added that it would be a good idea to remove the oven rack from over the hot coals when finished using it for cooking. It would be hot, so I'd need to be careful. Two pot holders were in the bottom drawer of the oven. I should use them when I handled the hot oven rack which could then be stored on the brick shelf in front of the fireplace until time to use it again. More wood could then be added over the hot coals.

■ ■ ■

I gathered my courage on MONDAY and asked Mike more about his personal life. "I had an older brother that I adored," he said. "Pete 'n I were buddies." He went on to tell me some of the things they had done together. "I was devastated when he died while servin' in the army." I didn't have the heart to ask him how that happened. Mike went on, "I've felt bad that I wasn't able tah do the last thin' he asked of me. It was in next tah the last letter I received from him. He said he had a feelin' somethin' was goin' tah happen 'n he wasn't goin' tah be able tah follow through on it himself.

"On his last furlough home before bein' shipped overseas, Pete wanted tah spend some time in the hospital visitin' David---his very special friend he'd had in high school 'n kept in contact with ever since. Their classmates had nicknamed them Shadow 'n Echo because they were nearly always tahgether. Pete left David's hospital room when a nurse said her patient needed an injection tah help ease his pain 'n then time for a restful nap. Pete said he'd be back later.

"As Pete was walkin' down the hall, he saw a sobbin' lady all by herself on a built-in bench under a window. He couldn't help himself. She seemed so sad 'n lost. He sat beside her 'n finally jest took her in his arms. She clung tah him 'n cried some more. Seems her mother had jest died. The cryin' lady was all alone there. No family or friend had come with her tah the hospital when she arrived with her ailing mother. The mother died while her daughter held her hand. The grievin' lady said her mother had flown in from another country. They hadn't seen each other for several years. Apparently, the trip took too much out of the older woman 'n she had a stroke. Her daughter called an ambulance 'n rode with her tah the hospital. It seemed at first that the mother was goin' tah be okay. 'N then the worst happened."

"That sounds so lonely for the crying lady. It was nice of Pete to offer her comfort."

"Well, Pete finally suggested tah the lady that she join him for soup 'n a sandwich at the hospital cafeteria tah help her keep up her strength. She admitted it had been hours since she'd had anythin' tah eat. It turned out that the hospital cafeteria was closed. Pete didn't want tah leave the emotionally upset woman by herself. He told her that he had a thermos of hot coffee 'n a package of glazed donuts in his motel room just one city block away. It wouldn't be much of a walk. He explained it was a lot closer than the nearest restaurant. She thanked him for his kindness 'n leaned on him as he guided her tah his motel room. Pete asked the woman her name, 'n she told him tah call her Red. Her hair was that color, Pete added in his letter."

"The woman must have really trusted Pete to go with him to his motel room," I said. Mike nodded.

"Surprisingly, she ate four donuts. She hadn't realized how hungry she was until that first bite. Red explained that she hadn't eaten all that day 'n thanked Pete for providin' the food 'n coffee. The thermos between them was drained empty 'n she had a dry throat when she finished eatin' the third donut. So, he offered her what a friend had given him as a gift the day before. It was in his duffle bag that he'd take on the train the next mornin' when he had tah start back tah his army base. He lifted the cork from the bottle with an attachment included with his pocket knife. He was surprised when Red took two big gulps of the strong alcoholic drink. An unhappy expression appeared on her face. He suggested it would be better if'n she sipped the drink instead. She tried that 'n then smiled. She apologized for bein' so hungry, but admitted she 'n her mother had left home in the wee hours of the mornin' before breakfast. Red nibbled on the fourth donut between sips from the bottle. Pete sipped some too. They took turns drinkin' from the bottle. Red said she was gettin' too warm 'n unbuttoned her long raincoat. It wasn't raining that day. Pete supposed in the rush of things when leavin' to go with her mother in the ambulance, Red had reached for the first coat she could grab." Mike paused, wondering how many of the details he should tell Joan. Pete had given Mike the full picture in his letter as he wanted his brother to understand what had happened.

Mike continued, "Pete was surprised tah see that under her coat, Red simply had a thin nightgown. A bit later when she was sweatin' profusely, her coat somehow slipped off her shoulders 'n ontah the floor. She finished eatin' the fourth donut between takin' sips from the bottle. Pete sipped some more too. He started feelin' warm 'n unfastened the top two buttons of his shirt. Pete had adjusted the heater tah properly warm the motel room, but he suspected the alcoholic drink was warmin' his body too. He decided Red had taken time tah prepare her mother for the ambulance ride, but there hadn't been time for Red tah dress. Well, he be a gentleman 'n ignore what she was---or wasn't---wearin'.

"Red said she was tired 'n felt so sleepy. Would Pete mind if'n she laid down on the bed for jest a minute? Without waitin' for a reply, she slipped out of her shoes 'n crawled up on the bed. He noted she had a beautiful body. She curled up on the bed 'n started cryin' softly."

Mike observed Joan's facial expressions. They indicated she could vividly picture the scene. He felt relieved when she said, "Obviously, Red had too much to drink. She most likely wasn't used to drinking hard liquor. Poor Pete probably didn't know what to do with her next."

Mike nodded his head. "Pete decided he needed tah git some coffee for Red. He remembered there was a hot coffee machine in the motel office. He didn't want tah leave Red alone, but decided he'd be gone for jest a short time. When he returned she was sleepin' 'n he had a hard time wakin' her up enough tah drink the hot coffee. He'd taken his thermos 'n filled it. He was able tah git Red up 'n walkin. Pete's letter said he didn't know how it happened, but later they had sex. He hadn't intended or expected that tah occur.

"A while later, Red said she'd better go home. She thanked him for helpin' her so much 'n for his sympathetic understandin'. Neither of them mentioned the sex part, but both were very conscious of it havin' occurred. He gave her his military address 'n asked her tah write tah let him know how things were goin' for her. She put the slip of paper in her purse. He urged her tah promise tah write tah him, 'n she finally promised that she would. All he knew of her was what she said he could call her—Red. She said she would write 'n he'd know it was her because she'd start the letter with Dear Curly--Curly in honor of his curly hair, she laughingly added.

"When Pete was sure she seemed well enough tah leave, he used the telephone in the motel room tah call the front desk. He requested a taxi for Red. By then, she had put on 'n buttoned her coat 'n slipped her bare feet intah her shoes. She grabbed her purse, kissed him goodbye 'n was gone. He didn't know her name, where she lived, or anythin' about her. His letter said she seemed tah be in her mid-twenties, 'n she had long beautiful red hair with the complexion to go with it. He noticed she wasn't wearin' weddin' rings." Mike paused.

"She did write two months later. Pete had decided by then that she had lost his address. When her letter arrived, he was overseas on duty. It took longer for mail tah reach him than he liked, but at least Red had written. What she said wasn't too much of a surprise---that she was pregnant. She added that she was married 'n it could be her husband's baby. She said she had a son. Pete was upset. On her envelope, she'd used a post office box but no name in the return address. He wrote back immediately. She still hadn't told him her name. So, he addressed his letter tah Red at the post office box address. His told her that he was goin' tah name her as the sole beneficiary of his G.I. insurance 'n she was tah set it aside for the baby's use. He had what he called a gut feelin' that he was the father of this baby. He said if'n he survived his overseas duty, he'd come tah see her in person at a time 'n place of her choosin'. If'n each of them was convinced that he wasn't the father of the baby, he could change the beneficiary on the insurance.

"In his next to last letter tah me, he told me all this and when the baby would probably be born. He mentioned the date, 'n said babies might come two weeks ahead or even after the official due date. He asked me tah watch the birth announcements in the newspapers durin' that four week period. But, he never told me what the lady's name was. He said he'd tell me in the next letter if'n Red wrote 'n told him her name as he begged her tah do for the baby's sake. BUT, there were no more letters from him until the one he never finished. All I had tah go by was she was married, lived nearby 'n had a son. Oh, 'n she had red hair.

"Days later, I received his last letter. Pete had addressed an envelope tah me 'n shoved the part of a letter he'd written inside it. In the first paragraph, he said he was expectin' a call tah duty any minute 'n he'd have tah immediately stop writin'. He said the lady had given him her name 'n he'd changed the beneficiary on his G.I. insurance within an hour after gettin' her letter. He was on the verge of tellin' me her name when he must have gotten the duty call. Well, after his death, somebody was nice enough tah mail me the letter with a note sayin' why it was never finished 'n offerin' sympathy."

"So, did you find what seemed like a probable match? How many babies were born in the area during the dates specified?" I looked at Mike. He was frowning.

"There were ten babies that I read about. I investigated them all---that is, from the information given, I was able to find the parents. Most of them were listed in the local telephone directory. I was an authorized person tah sell magazine subscriptions for a certain company. I found that useful in some of my investigative work. I had all the I.D. 'n application papers I needed. If'n I got a subscription, I put it through tah the proper company. One way or another, I checked the parents of each one of those babies, 'n none of them had a mother with red hair!"

I thought about that a minute. "Well, maybe the red wasn't natural, but the color out of a bottle. Do you suppose that could have been the case?"

"I wondered about that, but Pete's letter said she seemed tah have the complexion of a natural redhead. I looked at the various mothers 'n carefully noticed if'n they seemed tah have different colored roots than what their hair showed. Maybe a woman was experimenting with different hair colors. One lady with brown hair seemed to have the right complexion, but she said this was her first baby. Remember, Red said she had another child."

"Well, maybe the baby's mother went someplace else to have the baby. It wouldn't be uncommon for her to go maybe to her mother's—the baby's grand-mother—for the last couple of weeks or so before the baby's due date, especially if the husband was away a lot. Or, maybe she moved?" I was trying to be helpful.

"Yeah, I thought of all those things. Finally, I jest gave up. 'N then, you came along. You have the same color of hair 'n eyes as Pete did 'n you seem tah have his smile too. My heart did flips the first time I saw you. In no way after that was I goin' tah have Black Crow give me the order of creatin' an 'accident' tah end your life. I had tah convince you tah do what I said so Black Crow would be content. Your life seemed tah depend upon that. Even if'n you aren't his child, you remind me of Pete. I was particularly interested in checkin' your driver's license for your birth date when I had your purse. It was close, but not in the time period Pete specified for the arrival day of his possible child. 'N then I saw the photo of your family in your wallet. Your mother had red hair. This all seems like quite a coincidence. Did she ever say anythin' tah you about maybe indicatin' your birth record father wasn't your biological one?"

"No, never! When I asked her why my hair was a different color from anyone else in the family, she gave me to understand I'd inherited it from some ancestor. She pointed out that I have brown eyes like my father and brother. And in case I got to wondering about it later, she assured me that she is my real mother and she loves me very much. I definitely was not adopted. I was relieved, though, when I found I had high arches in my feet just like hers." I chuckled. "I guess in the back of my mind I had wondered if I was adopted."

Mike had a serious expression on his face when he said, "I gave my word tah Black Crow that I'd create the endin' she required if'n I couldn't convince you tah do as she wanted. She'll tell me when tah set you free if'n she is happy with the results of her plan. Let's make sure we keep her happy. Now you know why I was such a grouch until you gave me your parole, wrote the letter, 'n later made the phone call tah Richard. It's VERY important tah me that you survive this affair involvin' my employer. I'll do whatever I cin tah make that happen."

"What you seem to be saying is that you think you might be my uncle. I'd love to have one of those. Neither of my parents had a brother. My parents came to this country after they were married. I keep using the term *my parents*. They are the only ones I know, even if Pete does turn out to my natural father. Only my Aunt Sarah of either of their families followed later, and she never married." I was still mulling over in my mind the implications of what Mike had just told me. "It's possible that Red's baby wasn't Pete's at all. I suppose you've considered that."

"Sure I have," Mike said scornfully. "I even tried tah find out who Pete's G. I. insurance went tah, but it was considered confidential information. I was left in the dark regardin' it."

"Do you have any children of your own? Are you married?" Now I had even more questions about Mike. What if he was my real uncle? Could that be possible?

Mike looked at me for a moment with sad eyes. "I was divorced five years ago. I was caught by surprise when my wife told she'd been unhappy for a long time 'n wanted out of our marriage. I don't know why I didn't notice that or how I failed her. Obviously, I did. It took me a long time tah git over the guilty feelin'---'n lonely feelings too. Maybe it was a good thin' we didn't have any children."

I asked how he met Natalie. That brought a smile to his face. "When I advertised for a secretary, she came tah the office for an interview. I was impressed with her qualifications 'n attracted tah her as a person. I hired 'er on the spot. It took several weeks before I started takin' her out tah lunch. 'N then one thin' led tah another. Soon we were seein' each other away from the office. She finally told me that her feelings tahward me were gettin' too personal 'n maybe she'd better just quit her job 'n stop seein' me. I admitted I cared about her in more than a professional way. Maybe if'n she left the office, we could keep on seein' each other. It ended up that she stayed on the job 'n we saw each other away from the office even more often after that. When I asked her tah marry me, she kissed me HARD. Never did say yes, but then, after that kiss, it wasn't necessary. We went tah the jewelry store tahgether tah buy her ring. I said I wanted her tah like what she'd be wearin' 'n thought she should have a choice in the matter. She looked at me 'n then smiled. Said that was one of the most thoughtful things she'd ever heard of a fiancé doin'. So often, he'd jest give the girl a ring 'n she'd pretend tah like it even if'n she'd rather have a different one. I would have given her a large diamond with a ruby on each side. It wasn't what she wanted. She chose a single diamond with a special cut that made the stone sparkle in different lights. She surprised me when she asked if'n she could buy my weddin' band if'n I'd like tah wear one. So, we chose our weddin' rings that day too. 'N she seemed simply delighted when I let her pay for mine 'cause I could tell it meant a lot tah her."

■ ■ ■

Mike was deep in thought for awhile TUESDAY morning, and then had a serious talk with me. He said, "Cutie, I'm not goin' tah be able tah protect you once we leave the cabin. I've been tryin' tah think of a safe place for yah tah be. I'm wonderin' if'n you would mind stayin' on my boat by yourself? I'd insist you take my gun so I'd know you could defend yourself if'n it was necessary. Blue Jay could take you there once he leaves me at the hospital with Natalie."

I paused as I thought about it. "Can you tell me more? What's your boat like? How big is it? And where is it?"

Mike was proud of his boat. It was evident in his manner. His voice was happy when he talked about it. "Her name is *Lucky*. Boats are always called her or she. I don't know why. She's a twenty-one foot cabin cruiser. She has a covered cabin plus a separate room with a bed. Across the stern—that is, the back of the boat—on a small deck there is a built-in covered place for things like the anchor, paddle, fishin' gear 'n stuff. There's an ice chest 'n alcohol stove inside the cabin. You should be comfortable there except you might git cold. The heater quit workin' awhile back. You could always wear your jacket. The only bathroom facility on board is a covered pot—called a commode—in a cabinet under the bed. You should empty it at the marina's restroom up by the parkin' lot. Oh, the boat is moored at Harold Marina. That's quite a few miles from where you live. The river is wide there. Some other boats are tied up at the marina this time of year, but they are usually left unoccupied. I think you would be safe thar. If'n anyone happens to be in the area, you should avoid all contact possible. 'N Blue Jay could check on you every so often. Do you think you'd be okay with all that?"

Because I was convinced that Mike was doing his best to keep me safe from Black Crow, what could I do except agree to whatever he thought best? I told him that.

Mike chuckled. "I remember one time when I took a friend out on the boat. When I asked him tah throw the anchor overboard, he did without fastenin' the end of the rope tah the boat first. Wal, I tossed out the sea anchor—that's a bucket with a rope attached tah the handle—after I fastened the end of its rope tah a cleat. Then I got out the hook with extensions tah the handle. The water wasn't very deep, so I was able tah git the anchor back. My friend never forgot the incident."

Mike grew serious and added, "If'n you do go tah the boat, I'd be trustin' you tah keep your oath, Joan, but I have no qualms about believin' you'd abide by it. I'll check with Blue Jay when I see him 'n make the proper arrangements. Okay?" Mike looked at me with a question in his eyes. I nodded my head. I knew I was agreeing to keep my oath if alone on the boat, and I was indicating that I wouldn't betray him. I'd be on my good behavior on the *Lucky* as well as agreeing that I would stay there until he made other arrangements. By this time, however, I felt I could trust him with my life unless there was an order for my death from Black Crow. Actually, that possibility did worry me, but I tried to ignore it the best I could. I was glad that Mike had said earlier that he'd give me his gun for protection while I was on his boat. It made me feel a little safer when I thought about being there all alone.

I hesitated before asking, "Can you tell me anything about Blue Jay since I'll be in his custody if he takes me to your boat? If I'm under his control, will he be likely to take undue advantage of me?"

Mike studied me for a moment. It was like he wanted to say something, but felt uneasy about giving me too much information. Finally, he said, "You cin trust him completely. 'N when I turn you over tah him, I want you tah pledge tah him the same things you promised me about your parole. 'N yet, if'n he tells you one thing 'n I tell you tah do somethin' different, remember your first allegiance is always tah me. My orders will always override his if'n there is a conflict between the two. Agreed?"

"That seems fair. I agree." I was answering the part about Mike's orders always taking first place over Blue Jay's, but I realized too late that I had not stipulated that. When I said I agreed, it was to also giving my parole to Blue Jay. Well, Mike would likely have kept after me about that subject anyway. I was trying to give myself an excuse for not being more careful regarding the wording of what I had just promised. It was too late to worry about it after the fact. I decided that Mike was thinking of me as a prisoner again, but he was trying to keep me safe. I sighed.

"On a different subject," I said, "I see there are supplies on hand necessary for making fudge. If I can get the fire to boil the ingredients, would you like a special treat?" By then the propane tank was empty, and we were relying on the fireplace for heating our food. Mike's bright smile was good to see. "Fudge," I continued, "is one of my favorite things to eat. I'll make a small batch and see if it works out. Okay?" He nodded his head.

The fudge didn't turn out like I expected. Probably it was because I'd skimped on the amount of sugar I used since the supply of that was low. I was disappointed that my fudge was such a failure until I remembered long ago when my mother dribbled chocolate syrup over ice cream. I decided it might work if I poured my dismal fudge over snow. Mike looked intrigued when I suggested it, but he agreed that it wouldn't hurt to try. I felt like a little kid when I took an empty large bowl out on the porch and filled it with newly dropped snow. I brought the filled bowl back into the cabin. When I dribbled the syrupy fudge over the snow, it hardened. Mike and I enjoyed it as we twisted thin strands over our fingers and then licked them.

■ ■ ■

WEDNESDAY afternoon, Mike asked me why Unicorn Organization members can be counted upon not to break their oaths. I hesitated before saying too much as part of the membership initiation was about that, and all of the initiation procedures were supposed to be kept secret from non-members. Finally, I said, "It's hard to explain. The only time I've ever heard of such an oath being broken was about a year ago. Did you see the article in the newspaper where a man jumped to his death rather than face the consequences of breaking his oath?" Mike shook his head. I continued, "Seems he was in financial services, and one of his clients was skeptical of a particular investment the man urged her to place her money into it. He would earn a huge commission if he could induce her to invest in it. The lady asked if he'd checked it out thoroughly. Would he be willing to place his own money into it? He said he would. He pledged his word as a member of the Unicorn Organization that it was a sound investment. And so, she trusted him and lost thousands of dollars. When she complained to a friend who, unknown to her, happened to be a member of the Unicorn Organization, word got back to Unicorn headquarters. Immediately, the financial service agent was contacted by phone at his home. He was asked when it would be convenient for an investigative committee from the Unicorn Organization to interview him to discover the facts. This, the newspaper article said, was standard procedure for the organization if a member's oath appears to have been broken. The man was frightened and left home. He paid in cash and used a false name when he registered at an out-of-town hotel. (In those days, it was easy when paying in cash to register without providing identification.) When the Unicorn Organization committee discovered he was gone, the man's picture was circulated to all of the Unicorn members in the city and surrounding areas. It turned out that the man was recognized by the Unicorn member clerk at the hotel where the man had gone. The clerk notified the Unicorn Organization at the special telephone number given in the circular sent to members. A day later, a committee of three Unicorn Organization members arrived and asked the clerk at the hotel desk to phone the man's room to let him know they were coming up to see him."

Mike asked if this was standard procedure. Careful how I worded my reply, I said, "According to what the newspaper article implied, it was. The man was writing a letter to his wife when the telephone call came. He added a final note to it saying he was guilty of breaking his oath, and he didn't want to face the penalty. For one thing, he felt it would be demanded that he pay the woman double the amount she'd lost, and he simply didn't have the money. The commission he'd earned was lost in a gambling game. He begged his wife's forgiveness, and said the committee was knocking on his door. Goodbye sweetheart, he wrote. Apparently, the newspaper article said, the man then opened the window on the tenth floor and jumped to his death. The newspaper article quoted the last part of his letter word for word."

"If'n he had the money, could the Unicorn committee force the man tah pay it tah the woman? 'N if'n he did have tah pay, couldn't the member have gotten a loan or somethin' since he didn't have the cash? Why would he have to reimburse the woman anyway?"

I knew the answer, but decided to keep Unicorn secrets as I'd been instructed to do. Instead, I replied, "A follow-up article mentioned that when the three committee men were outside the door, one of them knocked. It wasn't planned, but it happen that just then a maid was in the hall pushing her cleaning supply cart. An odd sounding yell came muffled through the door. One of the men asked the maid to open the door with her pass key. She hesitated. The man said the yell sounded desperate, so she knocked on the door herself. When there was no response, she opened the door. The window was opened wide, and the maid went close it. She screamed when she looked down into the street. Later testimony verified that the man had yelled as he fell. There were more details in the article, but they wouldn't be important to you."

"So, if'n a Unicorn Organization member's oath is reported broken, the organization steps in tah correct any problem created by that. 'N I suppose there is also somethin' the organization does tah punish the member. Right?"

I didn't mention the legal papers a member signs as part of the formal initiation into full membership in the organization. "The article didn't say," I hedged.

"It doesn't matter. I won't break my oath to you. It is totally and completely sacred to me."

"I believe you, actually I do," Mike told me.

I wished I was free of the obligation not to tell non-members about the beautiful ceremony of initiation when I became a full member of the Unicorn Organization. I'd never forget how solemn, memorable and impressive it was. The secret meaning of the initials U.N.I.C.O R.N. was revealed and why the single horned animal was chosen as the symbol of the organization. The solemn ritual that seemed to reach deep into my soul stated that an oath made on the honor of a member of the Unicorn Organization was a sacred obligation, indelible, and never to be broken. This was one of the key parts of the initiation ceremony, but I kept silent on the subject. I wouldn't break my oath to Mike and the later one to Blue Jay even though I knew neither would complain to the organization if I did. They couldn't complain without revealing the kidnapping, and neither would want to do that.

The electric power had failed by the time we had breakfast on Wednesday morning. Mike had told me before we actually needed it that I should take the kerosene lamp from its stand on the wall in the main room and where to look for its fuel. The lamp was placed on the table along with the wind-up alarm clock from the girls' room that I was now setting each night before going to bed. I wanted to be sure to wake up when it was time to add wood to the fire in the fireplace. When the kerosene lamp was turned off Wednesday night, the fire gave the room a soft glow. We still had some wood, but our stack was dwindling quickly.

Before going to bed Wednesday night, I made certain all my text books and my spiral back notebook were in my book bag. Mike suggested that I select some paperback books that I hadn't read yet from the supply he'd purchased in town. He thought they would help me pass the time on the boat. I added three of them to my big purse. I hoped all would go well the next day. Hopefully, Blue Jay would rescue us then. I was still concerned about Mike's broken leg. I was a bit worried about meeting my new custodian. The night sky looked clear, and there was no wind moving the tree branches when I looked out of the window before going to bed. I could see stars in the sky above—a welcome sight! It looked like Thursday morning would be safe for Blue Jay to come, but I was puzzled how he would be able to do it. Was the bridge still out on the road leading to the cabin? Was there too much snow to be able to tell where the road was and wasn't? And would the landmarks on Mike's map to Blue Jay show up under all the snow? When I looked out from the front door, I saw snow had covered the second step up to the porch. I said good night to Mike and then crawled into my bed on the floor.

Before going to sleep, I said a silent prayer. We needed help and needed it soon. The telephone and electricity weren't working. The propane tank was empty and that made the kitchen stove useless for cooking or heating water. Our food supply was getting lower. I was stuck here in the cabin with a man with a broken leg. Yes, we definitely needed help SOON! If Blue Jay couldn't figure a way to reach us, we were going to be in deep trouble. We were on the very end of a little used dirt road apparently miles away from town. A bridge was out between us and town at our last report. Besides, with the deep snow, the roads would probably be difficult to drive over even if they could be seen. Would the black smoke coming out of the chimney do any good? How was Blue Jay going to get to us? Yes, we needed help. I prayed even harder.

8

My second Thursday morning away from home dawned clear and very cold. Would Blue Jay come? It was a constant question in my mind. I prepared breakfast and washed the dishes afterwards. By then, Mike was using his makeshift crutch derived from the chair. He was able to hobble to his bedroom and bathroom. He changed to fresh clothes that morning. I wondered if anyone noticed that I was missing. Richard, Aunt Sarah and Mrs. Connor wouldn't consider me a missing person. Would Tom fret when I didn't show up at college for these many days? I had never told him where I lived, nor had I shared my telephone number that was still listed under my father's name.

"When do you think Blue Jay will get here?" I asked Mike in worried tones. "Do you think he'll be able to find us? If the bridge is still out, how could he get here?" I was alternating between biting my fingernails and rubbing the back of my neck by then.

Mike shrugged. "If'n he doesn't git here tahday, he'll come as soon as he can. We still have food 'n firewood. We'll be okay." He sounded calm. Did he actually feel that way?

I wondered what Richard was thinking. I could see him clearly in my mind's eye. Had he come back to my house to try to see me? I hoped after I was again free, we could get re-engaged. Would he want to after all those awful things I'd written in my letter? I still felt like crying when I thought of him, but knew I didn't have a choice about breaking the engagement. Who was Black Crow, and why was she insisting on my breaking up with Richard? Could Black Crow be Mrs. Seymour?

Mike interrupted my thoughts. "You'd better start puttin' the pieces of tire on the fire," he said. "We don't know when Blue Jay will need tah see the black smoke. Do it a little at a time 'cuz we don't want tah use it all too fast in case he's delayed. The tire has tah last all day."

"What would happen if the tire was all gone, and Blue Jay doesn't arrive today, Mike? Maybe I could get one of the tires off of a wheel on the van so that we could have black smoke tomorrow?"

"Don't fret so much about Blue Jay's gettin' here. He's quite athletic. I wouldn't be surprised tah have him knock on the door 'n say he skied in tah help us. He might even have a sled with him for me tah ride on. Or better yet, maybe he'll arrive with a dog team draggin' somethin' big enough for all us tah ride on. Very resourceful is Blue Jay. 'N when he gets here, I expect you tah remember you've promised not tah reveal anythin' about your kidnappin' 'n this includes the identity of my accomplice. Right?"

"Of course, Mike," I replied earnestly. "If he cares enough to rescue us, it would be a terrible way to show gratitude to later identify him as a kidnapping accomplice. I promise you that if it ever comes to pass that I'm questioned about my kidnapping, I will never testify against him. I will not identify either of you to legal authorities as being my kidnappers—or to anyone else without your permission. I thought you understood that. And yes, I remember I've promised that if it comes out that I was kidnapped, I'm to describe my kidnapper with the long black hair, beard, and all the rest that is written in my notebook. That won't identify you."

Mike smiled. "Are you all packed 'n ready tah leave? I've got my stuff ready tah go." I nodded. By then, I had returned my bedding to the bunk bed.

"Since the electricity is off, it would be a good idea tah pull the plug on the refrigerator 'n place the broom tah hold the door open tah prevent mold from formin'." I'd thoroughly cleaned and dried the refrigerator a day earlier when it was completely empty. "'N I'd appreciate it if'n you'd go outside 'n pull the switch tah turn off the main power." He told me where to find it. "There's a snow shovel snapped intah a holder by the back door. It would be a good idea tah shovel the snow off of the front porch. Probably the roof prevented a big accumulation there though." I wondered if Mike was finding things for me to do to prevent my worrying about when or if Blue Jay would arrive.

Later, I heated water on the oven rack over bright coals in the fireplace and prepared hot tea for both Mike and me. "I've been thinking about what you told me about your brother," I said as I sat down at the table. "Do you have a picture of him to show me?" After Mike had taken one from his wallet and handed it to me, I gazed at it. Could this be my natural father? I did favor him in many ways. I remembered that Mr. Williams was holding a large brown envelope to give me later. I wondered if its contents would tell me about Pete. I handed the photo back to Mike. I placed more wood on the fire. After I sat back down at the table, I said, "When I was at the attorney's office signing papers, Mr. Williams told me my mother had left a brown envelope to be given to me when I was twenty-five or married, whichever came first. Do you suppose I'll find the answer there about whether or not Pete was my real father?"

Mike looked startled. "Joan! That brown envelope could hold the answer I've been searching for. The amazin' thin' is I had a strange dream the night be-fore Black Crow called tah offer me her job. In the dream, I saw an arm in a long white sleeve with its masculine hand pullin' aside the coverin' over a large pic-ture frame. Inside the frame was a picture showin' a tree with bare branches–no leaves. This was on the left side of the picture. In the tree was a large black bird 'n from its beak hung a clear plastic bag showin' inside a huge stack of money. Under the right side of the tree, stuck in a leafy bush, was a large brown enve-lope. 'N beyond that—to the right of the center of the picture, Pete was smilin' while pointin' at the envelope. Then the dream faded, 'n I woke up with a start. There was somethin' unusual about that dream. It had a different quality tah it than a regular dream. 'N the image of Pete's smilin' face seemed tah hang in the air even after I sat up in bed. I shook my head 'n got up for a drink of water. The next mornin', the phone call came from Black Crow. I hadn't thought of dream again until now. WOW! It was as if Pete was preparin' me for what was comin', but I didn't understand the dream then. I hadn't connected my spur of the mo-ment code name for my employer with the dream either."

"This is very strange. What did Pete want you to do if you did find Red's baby, and it was his?" I thought the answer was an indication of what Mike's plans for me might involve.

"Pete wanted me tah keep an eye on the child 'n make sure it was okay if'n he wasn't around tah do it himself."

By now, knowing about Mike's dream, about the trust that Mom had waiting for me, and my resemblance to Pete, I felt fairly certain he had been my father. "So, if I am Pete's daughter, it seems like you are doing exactly what he asked of you now. After Black Crow releases me, will you still feel the need to keep track of me?"

Mike didn't reply for so long, I wondered if he'd heard me. Finally, he answered. "Cutie, I jest don't know at this point. You are an adult now 'n once you are free of Black Crow, I'm not sure you'll need lookin' after. Let's wait 'n see what's in your mother's brown envelope. By then, you 'n me will both know more what the situation is."

I nodded my head as I was debating what it would mean to me if Pete turned out to be my biological father. What about the man I'd called Dad all these years. He loved me dearly, and I loved him back. Nobody could take his place no matter what some document might show on paper. Dad had been my active father. Nothing could change that. I might call Pete my father, if it developed he actually was, but my first and foremost male parent was the one I grew up with. I'd call him Dad no matter what.

I stopped even thinking about anything else when my attention was diverted by what in our quiet surroundings seemed like a loud roar overhead. Mike used his crutch to hobble to the door, and I was right behind him. A helicopter was hovering over Mike's van. I stepped out onto the porch. A man pressed his head against a window of the helicopter and pointed north. The aircraft went that way, and soon the sound stopped. All was quiet again.

"Is the back door locked?" Mike asked. I nodded my head. "Git your things 'n put 'em on the porch. You cin take mine out thar too. My suitcase is in the hall. Yes, 'n dump out all the water in containers 'n drain what's left in your bathtub. I didn't want you tah do all that until we were sure Blue Jay was actually arrivin'. Guess we cin let the fire in the fireplace burn itself out. We cin be ready on the porch when Blue Jay gits here. Told you he'd figure some way tah rescue us!"

We were too excited to stay inside the cabin while we waited. We stood on the porch wearing our jackets after Mike locked the front and screen doors. "I want you tah keep your eyes closed once we start tah fly," Mike said. "I don't want you tah know where the cabin is. When I look at you 'n blink, I want you tah close your eyes. I'll tell you when tah open them by askin' you if'n you're are all right. Agreed?"

I looked at him a moment before replying. I didn't think it mattered if I knew where the cabin was because of the promises I'd previously made about keeping things secret regarding my kidnapping. If it made him happy, it wouldn't hurt to agree. I would have enjoyed seeing the scenery though. I just nodded my head in answer.

"Before you leave tah go tah the boat with Blue Jay, I'll make sure you have my gun," Mike told me, "Be careful tah keep it hid as much as you cin while still keepin' it where you cin reach it easily. The under arm holster would work well for that."

"How come you'd trust me with it? Aren't you afraid I'd use it against you or Blue Jay? I just don't understand why you'd consider arming me with a gun."

Mike studied me for a long minute. "Actually, Cutie, a few days ago I would've considered it madness. I've been watchin' you. For example, you didn't take my gun from me when you had the chance. I saw you when you stopped with your foot above the top step of the porch while wonderin' if'n you were free of your oath about comin' tah my rescue. I could see it on your face what you was debatin' in your mind. I remembered when I had suggested you wait on the porch tah take things intah the cabin, you hadn't promised tah do it. I saw your face brighten when you remembered that. I could add more examples. My main concern is tah keep you safe, especially if'n you are Pete's daughter. I trust you tah keep your oath about not causin' harm either tah me or tah Blue Jay 'n that you'll not try escapin' from us while at the marina. I know for sure by now that you consider your Unicorn's word of honor as bein' a sacred thin' tah yah."

I wondered what dangers he thought I'd be facing. I was touched that my safety meant so much to him. "I agree," was all I said. By saying that, I was locked into keeping the gun while on the boat until he or Blue Jay relieved me of it as well as keeping all the conditions of my oath while alone on the boat. I asked what dangers he thought I'd be facing.

"What makes me feel uneasy is that Black Crow knows a lot about me includin' my vehicle license numbers. She didn't say anythin' about the boat, so I'm hopin' she doesn't know about it. Still if'n danger comes your way, I feel better knowin' you have a way tah protect yourself. 'N don't hesitate tah shoot if'n your life is on the line. It would be called self defense in any court."

I nodded my head. I was getting good at nodding effectively with all the times I was doing it lately. I felt uneasy, but decided to let things unravel one day at a time. We were still waiting anxiously on the porch for help to arrive. To divert the stress I was feeling, I glanced around at the pretty snow scene. I looked to see if I could spot the rabbit, but I didn't. Nothing seemed to be moving, not even a breeze. Everything seemed dead quiet, as the saying goes. Then I saw a figure coming up where the road ought to be. He was pulling a sled. As he came closer, he seemed familiar, but with the fabric hat that had a face cover, the big bulky overcoat he was wearing, and the snowshoes he was moving in a skimming motion over the snow, it was hard to be certain.

"Hello, Blue Jay," Mike said when the man came up to the porch steps. "Boy, are we glad tah see you!"

"Sorry it took me so long," Blue Jay answered with his distinctive accent. "I hope you can manage it, but I told the pilot that you'd pay him for the flight. I don't have the cash to do it. Sorry. I was able to convince him that it was an emergency. He said he'd trust me to make certain he did get paid eventually anyway." Mike nodded his head. Blue Jay studied Mike with the make shift crutch. Finally, Blue Jay said, "Well, I guess we'd better get going. I suppose we'd better get you settled first, and then I'll come back for Joan. We'd better leave the crutch behind as the space on the helicopter is limited, and you'll likely get a new set when we arrive at our destination." Mike gave his keys to Blue Jay who placed the crutch inside the main room, relocked the front and screen doors, and then returned the keys to Mike. It took Blue Jay and me both to get Mike down the steps and onto the sled. "I'll be back shortly," Blue Jay said to me as he gave Mike a knitted cap with face protector. "I realize you'll probably want to hide your identity," he explained to Mike. Once he was wearing it, the face protector did adequately hide Mike's features.

Soon I was all alone. *They wouldn't just leave me here, would they? The house and both the regular shed and the smaller tool one are locked. The air is freezing cold. Without any survival gear, I'll be in real trouble if abandoned.* It was a HUGE relief when I saw a figure headed in my direction.

Blue Jay was pulling the empty sled when he returned. He was carrying an extra pair of snowshoes under one arm. He pulled a blue knitted cap with face protector from his pocket. "Better wear this," he said handing it to me. "It'll help keep you warm as well as hiding your face. I brought you a pair of mittens too. I didn't know if you would have any with you. We'll load all the gear onto the sled, and you can wear the snowshoes to walk with me."

It wasn't long before I found myself seated aboard the helicopter. The doors were closed. Soon we were airborne, and Mike looked at me and blinked. I got his silent message, checked my watch, and then closed my eyes. The flight seemed to last a long time. I concentrated to keep my eyes shut. It was a relief when the 'copter landed. I was glad when Mike asked if I was all right. I opened my eyes then. I checked my watch and was surprised to note the flight had lasted just over an hour. I discovered a bit later that the airport where we landed was miles from my home.

Blue Jay thanked the pilot for a good ride and for his help. I noticed Blue Jay had pushed his knitted face protector up under his hat and was now wearing dark wrap-around sunglasses that prevented me from seeing his eyes even from the side of his face. A little of his black hair poked out from under his hat. I stretched. Blue Jay said he'd go get the car, and in the meantime we could be putting our things on the ramp so the pilot could take off. Mike wasn't much help unloading the luggage, but the pilot was. Mike took the pilot aside. I learned later that Mike paid the man cash for the flight plus some extra for the good service. It seems Mike had some of the cash from Black Crow in his thick wallet. The pilot was smiling by the time Blue Jay arrived with MY CAR! Then the sled, snowshoes and Blue Jay's suitcase were covered by a tarp and tied down to the carrier rack on top of my car while Mike's luggage and my book bag were placed inside the car. My purse hung by its double straps over my shoulder. Mike was helped onto the front passenger seat that was shoved back as far as it would go to allow space for his leg with the splints. When the pilot was certain all was ready for us to depart in the car, he shook Blue Jay's hand. The helicopter left, but very soon I heard the sound from it stop. Maybe it went to a nearby hanger or perhaps to a place for refueling.

"I called Natalie," Blue Jay said. "She should be at the local hospital by now." As we left the airport, Mike removed his face protector cap. From the back seat,

I followed his example and took mine off as well. It was only minutes more before we were parked in the emergency parking space at the hospital. "I'll go get
you a wheelchair, Mike," Blue Jay said. He left the car with its engine idling to
keep the heater running inside the vehicle. When he started walking towards the
building, I saw puffs of white as he breathed into the cold air.

After Blue Jay was out of sight, Mike took off his jacket and removed
the shoulder holster while carefully keeping his hand on the gun during the
process. He took the bullets out of the gun and put them in his pocket. He
smiled at me and said, "Take off your jacket 'n then come around and stand
by my open door." When I was there, he showed me how to adjust what he
called the harness that holds the holster in place on a body. After that, he
showed me how to make sure the gun would stay securely inside the holster
when not in use and how to access it rapidly if I needed to use the gun. When
he was completely satisfied I knew how to do everything correctly, he smiled.
Next, he had me put on the holster harness. He made certain it was adjusted
correctly for my body. He had me practice reaching for the unloaded gun in
the holster and then rapidly pretending to use it. When he was at ease about
my ability to do that, he handed me the cartridges from his pocket and said
for me to load the pistol. He watched and seemed pleased that I knew how
to do that correctly. I was careful not to point the gun at him during the
reloading process. When he noted I seemed proficient with the revolver, he
was satisfied that I knew how to handle it. Mike insisted that I place the gun
in its holster and secure it there myself to make sure I could do it correctly
when alone. When I was armed with the loaded gun, he double checked
to make certain all was done in the correct way. When he was satisfied, he
reached into his jacket pocket and handed me a small box. When I looked,
I discovered it contained cartridges for the gun. Mike smiled at me. "You
cin put it in your big purse. If'n you still feel bad about takin' my pistol, just
consider what the doctor would say if'n I was wearin' it when he examines
me. You could think of it as a favor tah me tah keep it until either Blue Jay
or me asks for it back. 'N you don't need tah mention the gun tah him unless
you want to. It doesn't matter tah me if'n he knows you have it or doesn't."
By the time Blue Jay returned with the wheelchair, I was sitting again in the
back seat while wearing the gun under my jacket. Everything looked normal.

"Ready to go?" Blue Jay asked Mike. "You'll be glad to know that I checked with the receptionist, and Natalie is in the waiting room." Why did his voice sound familiar even though I couldn't remember anyone with that particular accent?

"Not quite ready," replied Mike. "I want it plainly understood that Joan is not tah make any telephone calls except tah one of us while in either your or my custody without permission from either you or me. Include that in the oath you're goin' tah give Blue Jay, Joan, in addition tah the other things you've agreed like not tryin' tah escape 'n the rest. Go ahead, Cutie."

I wasn't happy about it, but I didn't see any alternative. I raised my right hand with the Unicorn Organization sign, looked steadily at Blue Jay, and said, "I promise you, Blue Jay, that I will not lie to you while in your custody, nor will I try to escape. If I agree by saying yes, nodding my head or otherwise indicate agreement, I will obey your orders to the best of my ability while in your custody if it doesn't place me or someone in serious harm's way. I will not make any telephone calls except to you or Meadow Lark while in your custody without permission from one of you. If you order me to do something that doesn't agree with what Meadow Lark has told me, his orders will be the ones I follow while I'm a prisoner of either of you. I swear on my honor as a member of the Unicorn Organization that I will keep these promises to the best of my ability." I dropped my right hand.

Mike frowned. "You must promise never tah reveal his identity as an accomplice tah your kidnappin' 'n not tah give his description as such tah the police if'n the question ever comes up. You will never testify against him. Furthermore, that you'll be on your good behavior while in his custody. In addition, you will avoid as much as possible any contact with anyone at the marina except Blue Jay or me."

It was my turn to frown. I raised my right hand again with the proper sign while taking the oath about the additional things Mike required. He nodded his head and smiled.

"Aw, I would have accepted her simple promise to be on her good behavior while in my custody and not to try to escape," Blue Jay said with the accent that I had learned to expect from him. Then, looking at me, he added, "I promise you, Joan, that I will protect you from all harm to the best of my ability while you are in my care." I felt touched by his sincerity. "Will you stay in the car until I get back?" *What a nice way to phrase an order.* I nodded my head. He acknowledged my answer with a smile and then turned to help Mike.

Soon Mike was in the wheelchair with his suitcase on his lap. Blue Jay said I should keep the engine running on idle in order to have heat in the car. "See you soon," he said as he turned to leave. He was still wearing his dark sunglasses. Mike waved at me. I moved to the front passenger seat of the car and then decided that I should readjust it back to its normal position. After doing that, I placed my purse on the floor in front of me, but left my book bag on the back seat. I wondered what was going to happen next.

Here I was, sitting in my own car with its engine running, the key in the ignition, and nothing holding me from just leaving—nothing except being trapped by my Unicorn Organization member's oath. I wondered if I'd been brain washed about never breaking such a promise. I'd need to think about that. And yet, I couldn't bring myself to willingly break my oath. SOMETHING STRONGER THAN GOOD SENSE WAS HOLDNG ME.

When Blue Jay returned alone, he was still—or maybe again—wearing the dark wrap around sunglasses that completely hid his eyes from me. He opened the car door and sat down in the driver's seat. I felt uneasy. Now would begin a new chapter in my captivity.

9

I clasped my hands together. Then I crossed my ankles. I felt like I had butterflies in my stomach. The silence in the car seemed thick enough to touch. When we left town, I noticed that the highway was clear of snow, but there was some on the sides of the road. It didn't seem to matter to me. I was feeling too nervous about what was going to happen to me next to worry about details like snow. Finally, I asked. "Are you taking me to Meadow Lark's boat?"

"Not right away," Blue Jay answered with his distinctive accent. By then he had removed his hat, but he was still wearing his sunglasses.

"Why not?" I dared to ask.

"Best get you something to eat. And you might want to change your clothes. I brought a small bag with some of your things from your house. We'll find a place to eat. You can take the bag into the restroom and change, if you want." He tilted his head downward and off to one side as he turned to look at me for an instant and then kept his attention back on the road. While he was facing me with his head in that position, above the bridge of the sunglasses over his nose near his left eyebrow, I'd seen the little mole. I knew that mark! I should have recognized him sooner, but I had no idea to look for him in this situation. His black hair, the distinctive accent when he spoke, and the sunglasses that reminded me of a mask a bank robber might wear—all these things had created a disguise that had fooled me. But now, there was no doubt in my mind—IT WAS TOM JENSEN! I felt a sudden easing of my tension. Tom would never willing hurt me. I knew that for certain.

I was digesting the fact that it was him. Neither of us said anything for a bit. A car darted onto the highway from a side road. Blue Jay barely missed it. "I'd be more comfortable, Tom, if you could see while you drive. You almost got us in a wreck hiding behind those dark glasses."

He pushed the glasses up on top of his head. In his usual voice without the accent, Tom said, "I was hoping you wouldn't know I was involved in all this. I didn't wanta be, but I wanted you to be safe too. Meadow Lark said he'd been watching you and discovered how often I was in your vicinity. He could tell I was mooning over you. He took a chance and told me about his employer. He said he didn't have enough data about who she was to go to the police, so he decided to try to save you the best way he could. If he didn't take the job, he knew the woman would find someone else to do it. He said the lady was acting like a crafty crazy woman on a fixed mission. You'd end up dead unless you could be convinced to cooperate with her demands. He said he needed help to take care of things at your house, move your car and odds and ends. He offered to pay me some of the down payment he'd received, but I said no." Tom took a quick glance at me. "I was only trying to protect you and your possessions, Joan. I didn't believe him at first, but he finally convinced me."

What to say? He needed reassurance that all was well between us, I could tell. "It's all right, Tom," I said finally. "I know you care about me and my welfare. I'd rather be your prisoner than anyone else I can think of if I have to be one."

"Aw, Joan! I'm not thinking of you that way. Instead, I'm trying to keep you safe. I'll take you the boat, but first to a place to eat. If you want, we could stop overnight at a motel in separate beds. I won't take advantage of you, but I could see better where to go in the daylight." He was pleading with me. He wanted me to understand he was trying to help me, but it was a long way to the marina.

Quickly, I decided. "Yes, that would be best. It wouldn't do to get lost in the middle of the night. You've already had a long day too. And gee, suddenly I'm hungry!"

The tension in the car evaporated. We ate at a small roadside restaurant. In spite of the great tasting meal, I suddenly had a sour feeling in my stomach. "How long ago did Mike talk to you about Black Crow and my kidnapping?"

"It was on Thursday before it happened."

"But, how did Black Crow know ahead of time that Richard was going to give me the engagement ring and how did she know when he had? This complicates things. Who knew he was going to propose?" I thought about that. Who had he told his plan? The only one I knew of was Claudia. Had she told anyone? Had Richard confided his plans to someone else? I felt a headache coming on. "It was the Monday night before the kidnapping when Richard slipped the ring on my finger. There's a missing link someplace if we are going to figure out who Black Crow is and what her final goal is."

Tom smiled. "I like that you said WE in that sentence. I'll try to remember more of the details Mike told me. For now though, please finish your dinner. We've got a lot of miles to cover before getting closer to the boat. The highway is good for quite awhile, and then we have several side roads to find before we get to the marina."

I elected not to change my clothes at the restaurant. I could change to fresh items after a shower in the morning at the motel. By then, I was convinced it would be better to rest awhile before going all the many miles to the boat. Tom had put in a long day already, and it might be hard seeing the various places where we'd need to turn onto different roads when it got dark. After our dessert of chocolate pudding, we were again in my car headed south. Tom and I talked about a lot of things including how my cat was faring. Conversation between us had come easy ever since I'd met him in one of my classes. We hadn't had another class together, but he managed to be with me often at college. I had gotten accustomed to that, and I felt rather empty if he missed one of his usual times of just happening to be where I was--an accident it was not, of course.

"After I leave you on the boat, Joan, I want to be sure you can reach me if needed. Do you have my phone number?" When I said I did, Tom continued, "Well, if you do call, just ask for me by my name. I've mentioned you to my Mom, and she wouldn't find it odd if you call." He paused. "Is it really true that you aren't engaged any longer? Mike said you had written the letter to put an end to it, and I did forward it on to Richard."

I looked carefully at Tom who was making it a point to keep his eyes on the road while driving. "I did write the letter, but it was forced. Apparently Richard didn't believe I meant it. Then, as Meadow Lark told you, Black Crow insisted I make that difficult phone call to confirm it. I suppose by now he believes the lies I told him. I guess technically, I'm not engaged."

"But you still love him and aren't interested in getting serious with anyone else yet. That's about the size of it, huh?" Tom frowned. His eyebrow and the little mole wiggled. Then he turned the car radio to a station playing symphony music. Neither of us spoke for awhile.

Fog rolled in about a half hour later. It was thick and driving became difficult. We decided to find a motel as soon as possible. We ended up in a room with two beds. That night came and went. It was like there was an unseen barrier between Tom and me. I did take a shower in the morning and changed into clean clothes in the bathroom. When I looked out of the window that morning, I noticed only light fog. Fog wasn't unusual for that particular area in November, but I wondered how we were going to find the various roads we needed to use to reach the marina if the fog got worse. Luckily, my car had a good set of fog lights. By then, I had decided that Tom had driven my car instead of his own as he knew I'd recognize his. He seemed to have assumed that I wouldn't recognize him while he was disguised.

We ate breakfast in the little restaurant next to the motel after we checked out. While we were eating, I asked Tom how he changed the color of his hair. He replied that he'd used a shampoo with a temporary color additive. He added that the accent he'd used to disguise his voice had come from when he was a boy and mimicked the speech of his grandpa who had come to this country as an adult. Tom consulted the map Mike had given him. He didn't look happy. When we were in the car and travel-ing in a general southerly direction, Tom asked me to look for a road sign--Matthew Road. He told me that is where we should turn west, to our right. He thought at the speed we were driving, it would take about twenty minutes to get there. That turnoff was at a "Y" in the highway, so we had no trouble seeing it. After we went a few miles, Tom said to look next for Edith Park Road off to the left. As it happened, he saw the sign before I did. According to Mike's map there were four more side roads we needed to locate. We missed seeing two of the signs in the fog and wasted time when we realized we'd gone too far and had to backtrack.

We did finally arrive at the marina. By then, I didn't see any snow in the sur-rounding area. We'd stopped en route for lunch and also for groceries for me to have while on the boat. The fog had become thicker. I suppose that was due to being close to the river. The marina parking lot was at the height of the road, but to reach the boats, a person needed to go down about twenty steps to the dock. Before we started down the steps to reach Mike's boat named *Lucky,* Tom pointed to a pay telephone booth. He made sure I had lots of coins in order to use that phone.

"If something happens that you find a need to leave the boat, you could hide behind the tall fence at the edge of the parking lot that conceals the garbage cans. Maybe you could hunch down behind the cans if for some reason you need to be out of sight. I can't imagine what would cause you to need to know that, but just in case…..." Tom looked at me with a worried expression. "I really don't like leaving you here all by yourself, but I don't know what else to do right now. Mike seems to have a plan, and all I can do is try to work with him. If you get scared, call me. In fact, you should call me every evening about five-thirty before I leave to go to my job to let me know you are okay, and I could tell you if there are any changes that you need to know. It would be great if Black Crow says her plans are all completed, and you can go home. In the meantime, I expect you to keep your safety in mind and to follow your sense of right and wrong in what you do while here alone."

"Tom, I need to give you a check dated when I disappeared from home. You can get a photocopy of it to show that you have the right to be on my property should anyone else ask. I'll write on it something about this being for mowing my lawn, taking care of my cat, etc. while I'm away. You'll need to buy more gasoline for the lawn mower, cat food for Fluffy, and who knows what else. I won't feel right if you don't accept my check. Cash it and use it. Be sure to get a photocopy of it first. That way, if you are accused of trespassing at my house, you'll have something to show that you are doing me a favor at my request. Hopefully, there'll be some extra in the check to help pay for things like this trip taking me to the boat and miscellaneous things you've been doing in my behalf. I really appreciate all you've been doing for me."

Within minutes, we carried all the things I was to have onto the boat. Tom had the key to the sliding door and gave that to me before he left. He kept hesitating, but finally said he'd better go. He did take my check with him after some protest, but I insisted. After he was gone, I worried about him driving in the now dense fog. I ate a cold sandwich and drank the soda pop that Tom had purchased for me at the last service station stop. I sat at the table and felt terribly alone after eating. Time seemed to stand still and before I expected it, it was dark inside the boat. I used the little flashlight from my purse and found the bed Mike had mentioned. I decided to worry about tomorrow when it arrived and went to bed. It took a long time to get warm. I heard a clanging noise that sounded nearby. The fog seemed to have fingers that edged through the sides of the boat and created a feeling of dampness inside. I thought the night was never going to end, but I did eventually fall into a fretful sleep.

10

Time seemed to go by slowly. Another Saturday arrived---my second one from home---and it turned out to be another foggy day. I drank my hot chocolate and ate cold cereal with milk while seated at the table in the boat. I was glad Mike had told me how to operate the alcohol stove. Tom had made sure I had a gallon jug of drinking water. He said I could refill it at the marina's faucet when needed. After cleaning the dishes and dusting the main cabin, I felt restless. I unlocked the sliding door of the cabin and walked out onto the boat's canvas covered rear deck. The canvas cover was fastened at the top edge of the cabin. From there, the canvas sloped down and was held in place with snap-on fasteners just in front the safety rail at the back of the boat. This was on a ledge a little above the storage container used for fishing gear and other things. There was a thick plastic window in the canvas partway down the slope. And, there were canvas side flaps on both sides of the boat going down to the ledge at the top of the hull which was about three feet above the deck at that location. The canvas side flaps were also secured with snap-on fasteners.

I noticed a framed bracket attached to the outside wall of the cabin. I looked closer. It was the registration for the boat. It gave the owner's name and address. I went back into the cabin and retrieved my notebook. I wrote down the registration information in shorthand. The owner was listed as Michael-- and even now I don't feel free to mention his last name-- and his address was given. I knew with this new information I could look up his number in a telephone directory if it ever became necessary. His home phone might be unlisted, but his office one would likely be in the yellow pages as well as in the white ones. I could always leave a message with his secretary if he was out of the office. I had a way of reaching Mike if needed which gave me some peace of mind.

I decided to go for a walk on the main wooden walk of the dock. No one could see me from the parking lot due to the fog. I went towards the main river channel this time. The *Lucky* was moored at the second short finger-like extension of the dock from the main river. At the end of the dock, I saw a ladder leading down into the water. About fifteen feet in the water from the end of the dock was a buoy with a flashing yellow light on top. Underneath the light was sort of a bell. I realized that was the source of the clanging noise that came when the water was rough due to the weather or from the wake of a passing boat. Why wasn't that term called *big ripples* instead of a *wake*? Oh well, what difference did it make?

I came back to the *Lucky* and climbed down the short ladder hooked over the narrow ledge on the right *(starboard)* side of the boat. The ladder's steps were on the inside of the boat behind the cabin. I stood on the wooden back *(stern)* deck. I had remembered to wear my tennis shoes that Tom had brought from my home. Mike had asked that leather shoes not be worn on his boat. I knew there must be a reason for that, but I didn't stop to figure out why. I refastened the canvas on the side of the boat and went into the main cabin. I marveled how compact and efficient the living accommodations were in the boat. I felt honored that Mike trusted me with his prize possession. I found myself wondering if what was in my mother's brown envelope would tell whether or not Mike was actually my uncle.

After lunch, I sat at the table with my back facing towards the stern of the boat. It felt like my brain was fatigued from all the studying and worrying I'd been doing in recent days. I felt lonely and quite depressed. It was Aunt Sarah's birthday, and I didn't feel free to phone her. I always phoned her on this special date. And this time I felt like I couldn't. I could have done it if I hadn't promised not to make any telephone calls without permission from either Tom or Mike. I hadn't thought ahead of time to ask Tom about it. I was being held a prisoner for as long as Black Crow demanded. If it struck her fancy, she could order my death. This had gone on for days and days. Actually, it felt like weeks and weeks. Time had moved slowly. She had taken Richard away from me after I had just found what it felt like to be happy again. My family was gone, and now Richard was too. Added to all that, I had doubts that persisted about Aunt Sarah. Could she be Black Crow? Richard could have phoned her before giving me the ring. He was old fashioned in some ways. He couldn't ask my father for permission to marry me, and Aunt Sarah was the next best thing. I doubted he'd done that though. I missed Richard so much it hurt, and Black Crow stood between us.

It was like I was a little mouse in a trap, and Black Crow was a cat eyeing me. All she had to do was push in the one way door on the cage and hold it open with one paw while she grabbed me with the claws of her other paw. It seemed to me that she knew exactly what to do, but she was enjoying the anticipation and watching me squirm.

I felt despondent and totally helpless. I wasn't in control of my life. I was in a deep depression, and the hovering fog made it worse. I felt like I was in a black pit, and the pit was getting deeper and deeper. I had no idea how to change things. I was frantic worrying about what might happen next. My sense of reality was getting warped. I WANTED TO GO HOME! What had I done to deserve all this?

I was feeling sorry for myself. And I was scared. I felt totally alone in a black world. I NEEDED HELP REALLY, REALLY BADLY. I leaned over and placed my head on my folded my arms on the table and gave way to tears. I started praying more fervently than I ever had before. *"PLEASE HELP ME,"* I asked earnestly. The prayer was heartfelt and sincere. It was as if my whole self was pleading and somehow knew my prayer would be received. It's hard to explain in mere words.

I remembered hearing someplace that once a sincere prayer is made, relax and give it to the Almighty to take care of. I felt inwardly exhausted, and I didn't think to do that. Instead, I was feeling extremely depressed and stopped thinking about anything other than my misery. I cried some more. I was startled when my attention focused on something else.

There was a bright light coming from under the seat cushion upon which I was sitting. *What is causing that?* The light was getting brighter. I thought maybe something had caught fire. I got up and raised the lid to the compartment under the seat. I tried to see where the bright light was coming from. *Oh, it's under the life preservers.* I lifted those out of the way. What I saw was a round glass ball about the size of a cantaloupe with what seemed almost like flames coming out of it. Well, I didn't want the boat to catch fire. I reached in and grabbed the ball. It was warm and when I stood, it slipped out of my hands. I watched what seemed to be a crystal ball as it rolled across the floor towards the bedroom door. When it stopped rolling, an even brighter light emitted upward. I pushed the cushioned seat lid down over the compartment and dropped down on it where I'd been sitting. I must be imaging what my eyes were telling me. I couldn't seem to stop looking at the scene before me.

The bright light turned into gray smoke that went up nearly to the ceiling. In the smoky haze, I saw a figure forming. *WHAT?* I rubbed my eyes. When I looked again, a man in a white robe with a wide shinny sash at his waist was looking at me with what I sensed were kindly intentions. I couldn't clearly make out his facial features, nor did I see his feet below the robe. I felt his vivid gaze. Somewhere in the center of my head, I seemed to hear his voice. "Don't be afraid, Joan," it said in kind, warm tones. "I'm here to help you. And yes, I created an illusion to catch your attention. You wouldn't have been able to receive the help you need from me in the usual way."

GULP! I was barely able to breathe.

"You wear your watch on your left wrist, so point your right one towards me."

HUH? This isn't real. My thoughts must be going wild.

"Joan," the voice commanded, "hold out your right hand." It felt like my right hand moved by itself. My index finger pointed towards the figure. I started thinking of him as Smoke Man. It was then that he waved his right hand over my wrist, and I felt something forming. I stared and saw a bracelet getting more and more solid. It was gold colored with a wide white band across the top. "You will heed what the bracelet says from time to time," Smoke Man told me. "The bracelet will disappear at the end of the parole you have given to Michael and to Thomas. You are not to mention the bracelet to anyone while it is on your wrist. You are the only one who will be able to see it. Remember, Joan, obey instantly if the bracelet tells you to do something. It may save your life. Peace to you." Smoke Man disappeared as the foggy gray smoke drifted away.

I had a headache. I went into what I called the bedroom, slid out of my shoes, and hid under the blankets of the bed. *I must be losing my mind. This can't be real!* I uncovered my head and stared at the ceiling. *Okay, I'm in bed. I had an interesting dream. Not to fret. Not to worry. It was just a dream!* That was when I felt a tingling on my right wrist. I rubbed the spot, and the tingling got worse. Curious and a little aggravated that the tingle had become an itch sensation which was becoming almost painful, I pulled my hand out from under the blankets to see what the problem was.

I discovered the itch was coming from under the bracelet. I felt bewildered. The itch sensation went away as I viewed the white top of the bracelet. RELAX, the word printed there said. That word disappeared and new words came. I'M HERE--and those words disappeared and new ones appeared--TO HELP YOU.

Then, I seemed to hear Smoke Man again in the center of my head. "You might not always sense my words," he said, "but you can see the messages in the bracelet after feeling the tingling of their arrival. I've made certain you'll sense the tingle. You'll be all right. It will take time for your life to settle down. In the end, what is to come will meet with your approval. Be patient. Your happiness will come in time." And with that, he seemed to have left me.

I wished I could sit down and eat a huge chocolate candy bar and a big bowl of vanilla ice cream. Those were among my comfort foods. None of those were available. I decided to take a walk on the wooden walk of the dock. There was no one around. The fog would keep me from view of anyone looking from the parking lot. I needed to do something to settle my nerves.

I looked more carefully at my surroundings as I walked away from the boat towards the shore. I saw the long walk of the dock had short extensions leading off from it. Boats were moored beside the extensions. Finger docks, I found myself thinking of them. Then I recalled that Mike referred to the water between the finger docks as *slips*. I saw there was a place for one boat on each side of the finger docks. Mike had said that there was a wide curve of the river where the marina was located. The curve had created what could be compared to a small lake beside the main river. I looked down into the water and guessed it was probably about six feet deep. I presumed the depth of the main river would be more.

I headed back towards Mike's boat. His was tied up at the side of a finger dock while the *Holiday* in the same slip was closer to a different finger dock nearer to the parking lot. On the other side of the finger dock---towards the river---where Mike's boat was moored was a craft named *My Dream*. The boat sharing the finger dock near the *Holiday* had a painted name on its stern saying *Playing Hooky*. I noticed that both the *Holiday* and the *Playing Hooky* had wooden hulls, but the *My Dream* and Mike's boat had Fiberglas ones. There were boats parked, that is *moored* as I heard Mike refer to it, in slips beside finger docks on both sides of the main dock.

I had nothing better to do, so I turned around and went further down the dock walk towards the parking lot. I noticed most of the boats had wooden hulls and outboard motors. Mike's boat and *My Dream* had inboard engines with gas tanks not visible except for the gas cap. I discovered that on the sides of each boat near the front and top of the hull was a boat number and near it was a decal. The numbers seemed to take the place of a license plate on a car while the decal indicated a year. I presumed the decal was similar to the affixed little sticker on a vehicle license plate to show the annual fee had been paid. I noticed that all the boats had their front ends---*bows*---facing towards the main dock. On my walk this time, I made it a point to check to see if any of the other boats were occupied. I discovered that I seemed to be the only person at the marina. I became aware that my nerves had settled back to normal, and now I was feeling more relaxed. I decided to do some more studying, so I returned to Mike's boat. I could even double check the two term papers I'd finished while at the cabin with Mike. It was a good thing that I'd written my reference notes in my thick notebook ahead of time.

Once back inside the main cabin, I replaced the life jackets in the compartment under the seat by the table. I looked, but I couldn't find the crystal ball. I checked the compartment under the seat on the other side of the table. The dishpan was still there as well as some bath towels and other items, but there was no other surprise like another crystal ball.

When it was the agreed time, I walked up to the phone booth and called Tom Jensen. He told me he planned to come the next morning and asked what I would like him to bring besides ice. I was expecting he'd ask, so I read him my list. Later, I realized that I had forgotten to ask Tom about my calling Aunt Sarah. I suppose it was because my mind was full of all that had happened that day. By nine o'clock that night, I was in bed and fast asleep.

SUDDENLY, I WAS WIDE AWAKE. *Something is wrong. What is it?* My bracelet was tingling against my skin. I looked at it. Where the smooth white place on top of the bracelet was located before, I now saw a soft white light and black letters that said, GET UP. I did and slipped my feet into my tennis shoes. To keep warm, I'd worn my clothes including my socks when I went to bed. I didn't wear my jacket then because I'd found a spare blanket wrapped in plastic in a cabinet under the bed.

Now what? I wondered. WEAR JACKET, the bracelet told me.

It was then that I heard two voices outside the boat. The dock lights were off for some reason. I saw darting lights of two flashlights as I carefully peeked through a crack between two drapes. A male voice said, "He told me the *Holiday* is moored near the *Lucky*." A flashlight beam focused on the stern of Mike's boat. "Here's the *Lucky*," the same man's voice announced. I saw both flashlights darting towards the boats near Mike's.

I heard what sounded like a teenager's voice say, "Yep, there's the *Holiday*." I remembered that was the boat moored in the same slip as the *Lucky*, but each vessel was beside a different finger dock. I wondered why the men weren't given the slip number. These were painted on the main boardwalk in front of each slip with the A and B positions labeled.

"Are yeh sure thar's nobody close enough tah get hurt when the boat explodes?" asked the younger sounding male voice.

"Nobody's around, son," the deeper voice said. "I agree with yah. I wouldn't 'ave taken the job if I thought somebody would git hurt. If it hadn't been the owner himself wantin' the boat damaged for the insurance settlement he'd git then, I wouldn't 'ave even considered takin' the job."

"Okay, what do we do first? Have yeh ever done this before?"

"Nope. The way I've got it figured, we pour gasoline over the back part and sides of the boat. The explosive charge will ignite it."

"Oops!" the younger voice muttered. "Sorry, I spilled gasoline on the wood walkway. Anyway, here's the opened gas can."

My bracelet formed words: PACK BAGS.

Backlighting from the blank message area of the bracelet gave me just enough light to see what I was doing, yet it was dim enough that it wouldn't be seen from outside. Hurriedly, I jammed clothes into a paper bag that groceries had been in. I placed my large purse on the bed and stuffed my leather shoes into it. I noticed that my box of bullets had drifted down to the bottom of the purse. I thought about the gun stored under my pillow. I removed my jacket. I properly placed the holster and its harness before reaching for the loaded gun. I made certain it was secure in its holster under my left armpit and then I donned my jacket. I checked to be sure all my books and the notebook were in the book bag. I looked around and decided I'd packed all my things. I placed my little flashlight in my pocket. I buttoned my jacket and pondered what I should do next.

A new bracelet message came saying, GO DOCK END. Those words faded rapidly. More words appeared, WHEN MEN LEAVE. Those words disappeared, and I waited to see if there would be more. Nothing else appeared, so while the men were doing something aboard the neighboring boat, I hurriedly gathered my things. Very slowly, I quietly opened the sliding door. I stepped onto the rear deck and listened carefully. Apparently the men hadn't heard me open the door. Quietly, I slid the door shut and locked it. I dropped the key into my purse. The men couldn't see me as I stood near the cabin under *Lucky's* rear deck canvas cover. From where they were, they couldn't see me through the rear window in the canvas either. Besides, I was standing in the dark except for the very dim light from the bracelet which I shielded so the light couldn't be seen from outside the boat. I prepared to unsnap the canvas on the side of the *Lucky* near the finger dock. This was on the opposite side of Mike's boat from the *Holiday*. I had the book bag and filled paper bag on the wooden deck beside me as I quietly waited to flee from the *Lucky*. My purse straps were hooked over my shoulder. Somehow, I never stopped to question what the bracelet said to do.

"All set?" asked the man standing on the finger dock next to the *Holiday*. "Ready tah leave?"

"Yep."

"We'll turn the switch back on for the dock lights when we git tah the parkin' lot. Everythin' will look normal until the blast. We'll be up in our car out of harm's way. I set the explosion timer fer five minutes. That should give us plenty of time tah git tah the car. We'll wait there tah make sure the blast goes off, then we're outta 'ere!"

GO B4 LIGHTS, instructed the bracelet.

I heard footsteps on the main dock's wooden walkway. When I knew the men were several finger docks away from Mike's boat, I unsnapped the canvas cover on the starboard side of the *Lucky* just enough to be able to lift a part of the side canvas out of the way so I could leave the boat. I placed my bags beside the boat on the finger dock's walkway, checked to make certain my purse straps were in place on my shoulder, climbed the short ladder up the side of the boat, and then stepped onto the wooden finger dock.

HURRY, the bracelet warned. I grabbed my book bag and the paper sack. I stepped up off the finger dock onto the main dock's walkway. I was afraid to run in the dark, but I walked as fast I dared using the dim light from the bracelet held low in front of me to show the way.   I didn't use the brighter light from my little flashlight in case one of the men looked back. I reached the end of the dock near the main river.

DOWN LADDER, the bracelet told me. Those words faded and new ones appeared, BAGS ON DOCK. The usual dim white light behind the words had a pink tinge that time. I had just gotten down the ladder when the marina lights came back on. In the rush of everything, I didn't notice until later that I had stepped down into the water a little above my knees. DUCK HEAD, the bracelet words instructed. I lowered my head and tried to breathe normally. My heart was racing. My breathing finally became steady. It raced again when a loud booming noise startled me. I dared to take a peek. A fire was blazing on the *Holiday*. In the glow of that, I saw smoke coming from the wooden finger dock's walkway close to the *Playing Hooky*. For whatever the reason, and I really didn't care what it was, it looked to me like Mike's boat was out of harm's way. When the blast came, the dock lights had flickered on and off and then stayed off.

GO TO SAFETY, the bracelet words instructed. I climbed up the ladder, grabbed my things, placed the purse straps again over my shoulder, and headed towards the steps to the parking lot. The fire on the seasoned wood finger dock beside the *Holiday* was widening. It wasn't on the main dock boardwalk where I needed to flee. In the illumination shinning from the fire as I walked past on the main dock, I could see the side of the *Holiday* next to the finger dock had a gaping hole. I wondered how big the explosive charge had been used to cause that. I saw bright spots of debris on the surface of the finger dock. I decided the explosives had been placed in such a way that the blast sent debris towards the parking lot side of the boat. I stopped walking and studied the scene more carefully. The *Playing Hooky*, on the opposite side of the dock finger shared with the *Holiday*, had a rope tied to the mooring cleat on the finger dock. The rope's dangling end was on the burning finger dock, and as I watched, I saw the rope catch fire. The dull glow of the flame was edging up the rope towards the boat. I wondered where the other end of the rope was. I could tell it was beneath the canvas at the back of the boat. Hopefully, there were no gasoline cans in the vicinity of that end of the rope. There were glowing spots on the back canvas. What to do? Should I try to save the innocent owner's boat?

NO, replied the words of the bracelet. GO TO SAFETY. Fear gave me extra energy. I again noticed Mike's boat seemed safe, but I didn't stop to check fully. I headed on the main dock's walkway towards the shore. I had just reached the bottom step when the electric dock lights came back on. I stopped and listened carefully. About thirty seconds later, I heard a car or pickup engine start. Then, I heard the vehicle roar out of the parking lot leaving behind the sound of flying gravel. The fire-starters were fleeing the scene

CALL TOM, the bracelet words told me. HURRY! I did. Tom said he'd come as fast as he could. I knew he was miles away, and it would take time before he could reach me. He told me to hide behind the fence and the garbage cans. I felt shaky inside when I sat on my book bag behind the last of three large covered cans. My energy seemed all spent. I felt exhausted. I started to shiver. The wetness on my feet and legs made me feel cold. The air was damp with a light fog. I sneezed.

I heard a loud BOOM and dared to stand up and look towards the sound. The *Playing Hooky*, on the other side of the finger dock from the *Holiday*, was burning wildly. Something there had exploded. In the process, glowing debris was floating in the air. As I watched, I was horrified to see a burning ember land on the back canvas of Mike's boat. It slid down towards the stern and stuck there against the back safety rail. Soon the canvas was on fire. I gulped as flames leaped higher. By then, the boat sharing the slip with the *Playing Hooky* was burning too. Weakly, I sat down. I was shivering.

Well, am I going to just sit here, catch a bad cold, and maybe get pneumonia? I can't do a thing about the burning boats. I need to take care of me. What can I do to get warm? Hmm. I have clothes in the paper bag. I could change my slacks at least. I used the little flashlight from my pocket to locate what I wanted. I ended up changing my slacks, removing my wet tennis shoes and socks, and putting on dry socks and my leather shoes. There weren't any spectators yet at the scene, so I was free to do whatever I chose. I felt more comfortable out of the wet items. I draped my wet clothes on the top and sides of a garbage can. My wet tennis shoes ended up on a different garbage can lid. I wished I'd taken a blanket from the boat, but I didn't. I ended up with a blouse covering my hair. That made me feel a little warmer. I read someplace that heat can escape a body through the top of the head. I sat on my book bag which kept my bottom above and off of the ground. I pushed my right hand into my jacket pocket. I discovered there the mittens Tom had given me as we left Mike's cabin. I quickly put them on. I wished I'd put the knitted cap with its face protecting option from Tom in the other pocket, but it wasn't there.

A car stopped in the parking lot. Soon, I heard a man's voice telling someone about problems at the marina. I presumed he was talking on the pay phone. A few minutes later, a sheriff's patrol car arrived at the parking lot with a siren blaring. Then, it was turned off. I could hear the radio contact between the officer and his headquarters. I learned the local volunteer fire department was being notified. I could see the bright glare from the fires reflecting in fog. I heard another explosion. I faced a long night ahead. Until Tom arrived, I was honor bound to stay out of sight to avoid contact with anyone.

11

Tom arrived just at daybreak Sunday. By then, the fire trucks were gone from the marina parking lot. The fires were out thanks to the special chemical spray the efficient volunteer fire department crew used. The owner of the marina was present and overseeing what was left to be done. He was able to explain to distraught boat owners what insurance the marina carried and also to be alert in case there would be a new fire outbreak which seemed unlikely. When Tom stopped in the parking lot, the marina owner was on the dock talking to someone who heard about the fires on a local television news program and was concerned about the *Playing Hooky*.

Tom knew where to find me. When he did, I gathered my still wet items and shoved them into the empty brown paper bag I'd kept in my purse. (I'd found over time that empty bags can be useful and I always tried to have one in my purse. Big purses are handy in many ways. I had a book of matches, a small pocket knife, band aids, safety pins, and a few other items in a small plastic box in my purse just in case I might need them someday.) I placed the book bag and the two paper bags (one with dry clothes and the other with wet items) behind the front passenger seat in Tom's car. We were able to leave the parking lot without being noticed, but not before I dared to look to see the condition of the *Lucky*. The fog was so thick that I couldn't get a clear view of Mike's boat. I was disappointed about that. I sighed when I realized I wasn't going to know how much damage the *Lucky* had encountered until later if someone could tell me. I knew several other boats had extensive damages. The fog had lifted somewhat during the wee hours of the morning. When I'd looked then while the dock lights were still on, I saw the *Holiday* had settled into what I supposed would be mud at the river bottom. Only the top of her cabin showed above the water. The *Lucky* was still floating, but I couldn't tell how much damage she had. Soon after that, thick fog rolled in blocking my view. I didn't venture going near the *Lucky* because people kept coming and going on the dock walkway.

"Well," Tom said when we were safely in his car about a mile from the marina, "you've had quite an unexpected adventure. I called Mike at his apartment. He's home now and Natalie checks on him often to make sure he's all right. I asked him what he wants me to do with you now. I hadn't expected his response. I'm to take you to stay with my mother and me. She's agreeable. She doesn't know about your situation, though, and I don't want her to learn of it. As far as she's concerned, you are to be simply a guest who needs a place to stay for a few days. Will you play along with this? You won't let her know the whole story?"

"Of course not," I replied sincerely. "We don't want her to be considered an accessory to the kidnapping even though, in this case, it was done with my safety in mind." It didn't seem to cross Tom's mind to doubt my simple declaration.

As we continued heading towards his home, the fog became even thicker. We decided it was just too dangerous to drive. We stopped at a little eating place until the middle of the afternoon when the fog was a bit lighter. Tom phoned his mother when it was obvious we were going to arrive much later than expected. He didn't want her to worry about our not getting there at the anticipated arrival time. When we did finally reach the Jenson apartment late in the afternoon, Tom introduced me to his mother, Mrs. Alice Jensen. I liked her immediately. The welcome she gave me was warm and open hearted. It was so different than way Mrs. Seymour had greeted me.

Tom excused himself after an early supper saying he had a job to go to. When we were alone, Mrs. Jensen took me upstairs and showed me the little den. She asked if I thought I'd be comfortable sleeping on the stuffed chair that extended into a bed. To me the warm, cozy room looked like a dream come true after what I'd experienced at the marina. *WARM*, I decided, was a great word! I assured her I'd be fine. She asked if I'd like to take a shower. If so, she'd let me use one of her bathrobes. She created the illusion of a substitute mother. I felt a place inside of my heart starting to glow.

After my warm shower and a borrowed nightgown, bathrobe and slippers, I felt a lot better. Mrs. Jensen and I sat and visited. She asked me about my family and expressed sorrow at my losing them. She told me some of her background. She wished she had space for a garden, but there wasn't any available at the apartment. I mentioned that my mother, Judy, enjoyed gardening and her love of roses. "In fact," I added, "my middle name is Rose." I said my brother's hobby was postage stamp collecting. Mine was reading. My dad, James, loved to golf. It was then that Mrs. Jensen told me her husband's name had been James too. She told me of his poor health due to heart problems and how devastating it was when medicines didn't help. She watched her beloved gradually fade away. She was especially thankful for family moral support when his death came. It turned out that Tom had two older brothers, Henry and Gerald, plus a sister named Mary.

We had a light late snack in the cheerful kitchen about ten o'clock. Afterward, Mrs. Jensen asked if I'd like her to put my soiled items in the clothes washer. I readily agreed. Would Mrs. Seymour have even thought of such a thing? I doubted it. I ended up still wearing the borrowed nightgown, bathrobe and slippers while my clothes were being washed and dried.

"It's getting late. I suggest ye go ahead and use the spare bed. We can talk tomorrow. I'll place your dry clothes on a chair outside of the den door when they are ready." Mrs. Jensen said this in such a loving, caring manner that I felt something click inside of me. Some lonely spot was being filled. I accepted her kind offer and before long was under a blanket ready to fall asleep. The closed door wasn't locked, and I had freedom to move around the apartment. In fact, there was a lock on the inside of the door that I could use if I desired. I felt honor bound not to leave the apartment without Tom's approval, but Mrs. Jensen didn't know that. I was totally welcome here. It was a friendly place, and I wasn't even remotely afraid I'd have that fatal so-called accident here no matter what Black Crow might want.

Yes, I'd be safe as long as I stayed in the Jensen residence. Tom had come to Mike's and my rescue at the cabin when we needed it. And I knew as long as I was under his care, I would be as safe as possible from Black Crow. I was so lucky to have a friend like him.

I wondered what Richard was doing. It was comforting to think he knew me well enough to believe I didn't really want to break our engagement and that he knew I truly loved him. *But, oh what will Black Crow do next? Who is she? What difference would my marrying Richard make to her?*

My mind was too full of questions going around in my head to sleep. Who was Black Crow? If I knew that, I'd probably know the reason for her actions.

Would Mrs. Seymour like to see me dead? Sometimes she had glared at me like she wished I was completely erased form Richard's memory. I knew Richard felt sorry for her due to her grief over the loss of her daughter, Laura, who died of acute leukemia just a year earlier. Richard didn't like talking about his sister, but he had wanted me to know the circumstances. I felt he tended to pamper his mother a bit too much, but I could understand it. I remembered a conversation weeks ago when Richard told me that his mother blamed her husband for Laura's death. Mrs. Seymour claimed her husband hadn't gotten medical care for Laura soon enough. I found myself wondering if Mrs. Seymour felt guilty that she hadn't done it herself and had transferred the guilt to her husband instead. Richard said he, himself, had talked personally to Laura's doctor about his sister's ailment and was told in positive tones that nothing could be done under Laura's particular circumstances to change the outcome. The doctor stressed that wasn't true in all cases of leukemia though. He said the earlier it was detected, the better, except in the very rare type that Laura had. Maybe someday, even her type would be curable with the advances of modern medicine. Richard had gone on to tell me that it was after Laura's death that his parents seemed to drift apart. Now, Mr. Seymour spent as little time at home as he could manage. I hadn't thought for weeks about what Richard had mentioned about Laura and the bitterness that had developed between his parents. As I lay there with various thoughts popping into my head, this conversation came to the forefront. Maybe it helped explain Mrs. Seymour's reluctance to accept a new female into her family circle? Nah, that was a pretty weak excuse. Mrs. Seymour simply didn't like me, period.

I needed to accept that in this world, a person couldn't be liked by every single other person in it. Nor could a person expect to like every person on the planet. Was it that I truly didn't like Mrs. Seymour, or was it her actions I didn't like? I yawned. Finally, I could relax and shut my eyes.

■ ■ ■

It seemed like only minutes, but actually it was hours later when I heard a gentle knock on the door. I woke up and said, "Come in."

Mrs. Jensen stuck her head around the door. "If ye are hungry, dear, breakfast is ready." I nodded my head, and she closed the door. Another day had started. I was in a SAFE place. What a wonderful feeling! Tom was seated at the table when I arrived in the kitchen. His mother was there too. A place was set for me. I slid into the waiting chair. The telephone in the hall rang, and Mrs. Jensen went to answer it.

"The last time I was at your house, I packed a few things for you," Tom said smiling at me. "I figured you could use some more clothes 'n stuff."

I nodded my head.

"I checked your cat. She's fine. I took my book bag this time. When I knew Mrs. Connor was watching, I removed three cans of cat food from it before going into the house. I still took the book bag with me when I went inside. Then, I stacked about fifteen cans of cat food on the kitchen table. That way, Mrs. Connor wouldn't be suspicious when I left with what she'd assume was the empty book bag. While I was watering the lawn, she came over and asked me about you. She figured you are still enjoying your trip. I told her I didn't have any news to tell her. After she left, and I finished watering outside, I gathered the mail from your mail box. I took it into the house like I always do—nothing suspicious about that. I've been leaving the mail on your kitchen table. I started putting everything except the obvious junk mail and the magazine you received inside my book bag. I noticed the stack of mail was in a slightly different spot on the table than where I was certain I'd left it. Either the cat had gotten up on the table or Mrs. Connor had been in the house. So I left all the mail on the table. There didn't seem to be anything that needed immediate attention, but I remembered there had been an electric bill from the first day I'd collected your mail. Well, today it was gone. I figured maybe Mrs. Connor took it to pay for you to avoid your being charged a late fee. She'd know you'd pay her back. I went into your bedroom to gather some clothes I thought you might need. I noticed a potted plant had been freshly watered. I hadn't done that. So by then, I knew Mrs. Connor was trying to be helpful. Rather than move your toothbrush, I decided it would be wiser to purchase a new one for you. I was going to be extra careful not to arouse any suspicions when I left. I wish I'd thought about using the book bag sooner to get things from the house for you. Before, I sneaked an item or two at a time to my car, so I could bring you the extra things at the boat. A nosey neighbor can be a nuisance at times, but a blessing at others. You can be fairly certain that anyone nosing around your place will get questioned by her. I checked to make sure the automatic light would still come on at night when it should. There was no burned out bulb or anything not working correctly. Makes it appear someone is there. I'm going to need to mow the lawn again before long. Maybe I'll take something in my book bag next time I go, and then I would be able to bring you something else you might want."

What a friend I had in Tom. I looked at him and simply said, "Thank you."

Mrs. Jensen returned to the table. "That was Mrs. Johnson reminding me of a committee meeting tomorrow. And then, we got to chatting. Sorry to be gone so long."

"After we take care of the dishes, would you like to go for a walk, Joan?" Tom asked. I nodded my head. After that, normal conversation flowed around the table.

We both wore jackets when we left the apartment. I wore the gun under mine as it seemed it would be what Mike would have wished me to do. The sun was shining brightly. No fog this morning. Tom and I walked in silence for the first two blocks, and then Tom burst out, "Joan, I don't know what to say. I'm scared for you. How did Black Crow know you were on Mike's boat? Does she have spies everywhere?"

I assured him that the fires at the marina had nothing to do with Black Crow. I admitted that I was concerned about what she'd do next. Hopefully, she'd allow me to be released and go back to living my own life again soon.

"But what if she just ignores you from here on? How will Mike and I know you'd be free? Surely, she'd tell Mike, wouldn't she?" Tom was frowning. "I don't like this mess one bit, but I'm glad you're here with Mom and me. This way, I know what's happening to you and able to protect you the best I can. Surely, Joan..." Tom stopped walking, so I did too. He paused as if trying to find the right words, and then continued, "By now, you must have an idea about how I feel about you." He reached out and held my hand. "I'm deeply in love with you. It's been so hard knowing there was no hope for me, that you're in love with someone else. You can't imagine what it was like when I saw your engagement ring."

I pulled my hand away. I turned away from him. His admission affected me deeply. How to offer sympathy? What to say? Finally, I turned back and faced him. "Oh Tom, I'm sorry I've been the cause of pain to you. I can't help what I feel about Richard. Yet, I treasure your friendship. I trust you completely. I'd miss you if you weren't in my life. How I can love Richard and feel so strongly about you, I don't know. I deeply appreciate how you've gone out on a limb to help me in this affair with Black Crow. I know you are risking a terrible sentence for being a part of my kidnapping. I realize it's because you care so much. I feel blessed that you do, but I see only hurt in the end for you, and I hate that. I can be passionately in love with only person at a time. I know you realize that. It's hard to explain, but I'd like very much to stay in contact with you and your Mom when this is all over."

Tom sighed. "I know. Yes, I do know. I just can't help myself and how I feel. Yes, I'd like to stay in touch no matter what. We can be friends if nothing more."

We started walking again. Neither of us said anything for six blocks. Then, we turned and started back towards the apartment. Fog was beginning to form. "What did Mike say when you told him about what might have happened to his boat?" I asked finally.

"He was sorry about that, but said the important thing is that you are safe. He has insurance on the boat. Material things can be replaced anyway. If something had happened to you while under his care, he'd have never forgiven himself. Like me, he wondered if Black Crow was responsible for the marina fires. He'll feel relieved when he learns she wasn't." Tom again reached for my hand. I didn't have the heart to pull it away. "Mike said he'd try to call you later today. I'll need to attend classes. I'll be lucky if I pass all of them since I've missed so many lately."

That caused me to think of my hope to try to take examinations in lieu of my recent many days of missed attendance in my classes. I wondered if maybe that would be a good solution for Tom if he felt he would need that option. After I mentioned that, there seemed little left to say to each other during our walk. The air between us seemed bittersweet, and there was a subtle sense of tension.

I excused myself once we arrived back at the apartment saying I would like to take a nap even though it was early in the day. I mentioned that I'd missed a lot of sleep lately. Tom nodded his head knowingly. Mrs. Jensen went with me to the den and made sure I had everything I needed. Then, she said sweet dreams and left me alone with my thoughts.

12

Mike did call me that afternoon. After Mrs. Jensen handed me the telephone handset, she left the hall and went into the kitchen. "Hello, Cutie," Mike said cheerfully. "Can you talk freely?" As I sat down on the low back chair by the small telephone table, I shook my head, then realized he couldn't see me. "Not too much," I replied. I wasn't sure how much Mrs. Jensen could hear beyond the hall and the open door of the kitchen.

"Then, I'll do the talkin' 'n you can say yes or no, or comments in short words. Black Crow wants you 'n me tah go tah a certain phone where she wants tah talk with both of us. I don't know if'n that's good or bad. Ask Tom tah call me when he gits home 'n I'll tell him whatever details I know by then. She hasn't told me yet where the certain phone is, but she said she would shortly. I'm hopin' it isn't a trap tah git us tah where she cin have us both destroyed in one sweep, but I don't think we have much choice. We cin take what safety measures we possibly cin. 'N be sure tah wear the gun under your jacket. Does Tom know you have it?" Mike was carrying on a one way conversation until then.

"No."

"Wal for now, best tah keep it that way, I think." Then he changed the subject. "Did you see who started the fires at the marina?"

"Yes, but not very well. I could hear the conversations though."

"Tom seems tah think you believe Black Crow had nothin' tah do with it. Is that right?" Mike seemed agitated. Clearly, he suspected she was at the bottom of it, and the implications were worrisome.

"I heard the main man say he was hired by the owner of the boat named *Holiday*, and it was to get an insurance settlement. I hope your boat is covered by insurance?" I remembered Tom had said something to the effect that it was, but I wanted to hear it from Mike himself.

"Not tah fret about it, Cutie. Yeah, the *Lucky* is covered by insurance. No boat will ever be the same tah me, though, as that one. I haven't been able tah go see the damage yet. Maybe there isn't much. Still, it's a material thing 'n cin be replaced if'n needed. Your safety is more important." I heard him sigh. "Okay, have Tom call when he gits in. 'N take care of yourself. 'Bye." Mike broke the telephone connection.

I hoped Black Crow was going to order my release after getting an assurance from me of some kind. She must have some reason to talk to me in addition to Mike. Oh well, I'd worry about it when I knew what it was all about. Obviously, I didn't have a choice about being there with Mike when she wanted to talk with us. I hoped she wasn't having the phone we were to use booby trapped. Later, after he had talked with Mike, Tom told me we were to go to the fanciest hotel downtown. In the lobby there, Mike was to answer one of the pay phones in a booth, and I was to answer the one in an adjacent booth. (In those days, pay phones were in booths with glass windows and doors that closed.) Black Crow was going to have a conference call with us. She would set a time for our being there and would let Mike know when a bit later. What went through my mind was, *And so now the plot thickens.*

It turned out that we weren't to go to the Hotel Elliott until the following evening. I was nervous in the meantime. *What was Black Crow going to tell us?* The time of the scheduled telephone call finally arrived. Tom was nervous too. When he and I arrived in the hotel lobby, we found Mike waiting for us. He was even more tense than either Tom or me. "I'm prayin' she won't end up orderin' that fatal 'accident' tah yah, Cutie. It's hard tah know what tah expect from her. She doesn't seem tah be mentally stable where you are concerned. I have no idea what she has against you." Mike was biting his fingernails. "Still, if'n it's the 'accident' order about tah be issued, I doubt she'd want tah talk with you. Maybe she wants tah hold that threat over your head tah convince you tah do somethin' you'd hate doin'. Keep your fingers crossed. Five more minutes tah go before the call." Tom didn't say anything, but I found it comforting that he was holding my hand.

I had the sensation that someone was staring at me. I looked up and across the huge room of the lobby, I saw a man in a single telephone booth talking on his phone. I was glad I was wearing the hidden gun under my jacket. The man seemed more interested in me than a mere casual observer would be. I wondered if he was working for Black Crow. The man studied what I suspected was a picture held in his hand. Then he shoved it into his pocket, turned his back towards me and talked some more into his telephone. Within a minute after he cradled his phone, we heard the ringing of the telephone in our nearest booth. It had seemed a terribly long five minutes while we'd waited for that.

Mike hobbled on his crutches to answer the telephone. I went to the closest other booth. I had just reached its door when "my" phone rang. Tom had followed me and stood close enough so he could hear what was said on the incoming call. "This is Joan," I said as calmly as I could. I turned so I could watch the man in the telephone booth on the other side of the big lobby.

"I want to talk with both of you," Black Crow said in what seemed like a self-satisfied tone. "I have one more demand to make of Joan, and then she'll be free of me." There was what might be called a pregnant pause. She let that register with us. "Richard is moping and is listless. He needs a definite ending to the engagement and a dashing of hope for any possibility of a reconciliation." Another pause for effect. "Here's what I want the two of you to do. What I demand the two of you do. Otherwise, Joan, you won't live to see the end of the week. And you, Mike, will be honor bound to do as you promised."

Well, she certainly stated the alternative if Mike and I didn't agree to her demand. Mike looked at me through the booth windows and shook his head in doubt and wonder. He might as well have said, "I don't believe this."

Mike seemed tongue-tied, so I ventured, "Exactly what is it that you want of us? You seem to have full control of whether I live or not."

"Yes, you little nobody," Black Crow said with a lisping voice. "I've got you just where I want you. If Mike hadn't objected so much to what I had in mind for you in the beginning, there wouldn't be the problem now."

"So, madam, what do you want?" I held my breath. The suspense was immense.

"You and Mike are to marry. And stay married! You are to send an announcement of your marriage to the Seymours, graciously accept what congratulations they might offer, and swear never to have any further contact with them. If Richard ever tries to establish any contact after that, you are to snub him firmly. If you do all this, I'll not interfere in your life, Joan, in any way, and Mike will get his final cash payment from me."

"Oh," I said in a hoarse voice. "Well, I won't do it!"

Mike interrupted. "Wait a minute, Joan. Let's talk this over."

Black Crow said gleefully, "Not much choice from your viewpoint, huh, Mike. I'm sure you can convince Joan she doesn't want to be dead." Then she laughed. It sounded like a horse neighing—and suddenly I knew who she was, and what the whole purpose of breaking the engagement was. She was Claudia's mother, Mrs. Phillips.

My bracelet started tingling. I saw the message—BARGAIN. Yes, I could do that now that I knew the why of my kidnapping.

"Let me 'ave a minute tah talk sense tah Joan," Mike said then.

I looked across the lobby. The man was still in the phone booth there. It was as if he was waiting for a call to come in. I wondered about that as I shook my head at Mike. I continued talking to Black Crow. "So, if I marry and let Richard and his parents know, that's your first requirement, right?"

"Obviously," Black Cow replied seeming to almost laugh at the words.

Tom pulled my arm. "See if you can marry me instead of Mike" he whispered. I nodded that I understood.

"You don't really care who I marry, just that I do right way, correct?" I was starting to get the feel of how this bargaining process should go to be effective.

"If you can find some fool willing to do that, fine. Mike will be off the hook." Black Crow was enjoying herself and her sense of power. "Hear that, Mike? Won't you help her look?" She laughed that horse type laugh again. I noticed Mike's face. It had turned quite pale.

My bracelet tingled. I saw the words, TIME LIMIT.

"Okay, if I marry right away, and agree to stay married for a year, would that work for whatever your purposes are?" *Oh, I know what those are!*

Black Crow didn't respond immediately. Obviously, she was thinking of the outcome of that idea. Finally, she said, "Yes, if you stay married for a year, a divorce would be acceptable. After announcing your marriage to them and acknowledging any congratulations or wedding gifts you might receive from any of the Seymours, you must not contact any of them as long as either you or Richard is married. He probably will be married before you are divorced. Furthermore, if Richard tries to contact you in any way while either of you is married, you must snub him in a way that will leave no doubt in his mind that you want nothing to do with him."

AGREE, said the bracelet's message place.

"All right," I said into the phone's mouth piece. "I can live with that."

"Live is the correct word, young lady. To make that happen, you must marry within a week, and let Richard and his parents know within a week after that. She paused. "And Mike, you must agree to this too if she doesn't find some sucker to wed her within the stated time limit."

Mike looked at Tom who nodded. "Yeah, I agree," Mike answered. "I'll make sure she marries someone, even if'n it turns out tah be me."

"Good," replied Black Crow. "Sounds like a workable arrangement. Still, I need some assurance that Joan will live up to what she's agreed. Mike, you vouch that she makes the Unicorn sign when she promises all these things on her honor as a member of the Unicorn Organization. I know that would be a sacred oath to her."

This time, I didn't need a prodding from the bracelet to know what the next step in my bargaining was to be. "Wait a minute," I said sternly. I dared to use that tone now that I knew who she was and what her purpose was. "I will take the oath you require, but only if you give me some assurance that this is really the last thing you will demand of me, that I will be free of you after I notify the Seymours of my marriage. And one more thing---that you will never cause harm to me or someone dear to me. And this includes Richard." Mike was pointing to himself. "Your hired man is motioning that he wants himself and his accomplice and their dear ones included in your assurance." Mike nodded his head and Tom squeezed my hand.

"Sure, Joan, I can promise all that with my hand on the Bible." She felt at ease now.

"But, I can't see you do that. Will you swear on the memory of your mother?" I knew I was taking a risk demanding that, but it was the only thing I knew that seemed sacred to her.

Black Crow sputtered. Finally she said in remorseful tones, "So you figured out who I am."

Before this could trigger her to have thoughts of causing me harm, I hastened to add, "But you need not worry that I will reveal it to anyone as long as you live. I'll pledge my oath on it along with the other things we've agreed to if you will make the complete promise I ask of you."

I knew the stakes were high, both for me and for what she wanted to accomplish. Tom held my hand tightly as the pause lengthened. Mike leaned against the side of his booth while holding his head in both hands. The silence lengthened. At last, Black Crow answered. "Yes, I promise what you ask on the memory of my mother. Now you must take the oath you promised to make. And, Mike, you must be my witness that she does it while making the proper sign."

I carefully worded the oath required of me. Mike verified that it had been done it in the manner she wanted. Mrs. Phillips told Mike that after my marriage was confirmed that she would send him his final payment. She added that she wanted to talk with me privately, that Mike should hang up his phone and leave his booth. A moment later she asked me if she and I could talk privately. I answered that we could. I motioned to Tom to go with Mike who was then sitting on a nearby sofa.

"I didn't expect all this to get so involved, Joan," Black Crow—Mrs. Phillips—told me. "After my hired man, as you called him, convinced me to let you live if you would do what I demanded, I felt more at ease about the situation. And then, things didn't go as I expected, and I needed to add more requirements to achieve my goal. I got so wound up in the whole thing that I couldn't seem to let go." She paused.

"I can see how that could happen," I said.

"It really isn't you that I hate---just that Richard loves you so much. I had to do something to break that spell. I know you can guess why. I do wish you happiness in your life, Joan, after you're completely out of Richard's. Maybe someday you'll be able to forgive me. I have every confidence that you'll do all you promised me. I will keep my promise to you as long as you keep yours. If you don't, I will follow through with my threat of ordering your death—and Richard's too if Claudia can't have him. YOU UNDERSTAND ME?" Her voice sounded like flint steel. I knew she meant what she said.

Will she keep her word to me if I do as she has demanded? Can I trust her promise? My wrist tingled, and I looked at the bracelet. YES, the single word said. I sighed. The telephone dial tone came on. Mrs. Phillips had ended the call. I had no doubt that she had become fanatical almost to the point of insanity about getting Claudia and Richard married. She would follow through with her threats if I didn't do as I promised her I would. I was sure of it.

As I turned to join Mike and Tom, I looked across the lobby. The man in the telephone booth was answering his phone. As I watched, he turned towards me and smiled. He gave me a half salute and blew me a kiss that I somehow sensed meant, *Congratulations! You won, and I'm glad.* I clasped my hands in front of my chest, bowed my head and wished him a blessing. I suspected that he'd been in contact with Mrs. Phillips and that she had told him he was free to leave without doing harm to me and whoever appeared with me by the telephone booths. He walked out of an exit door on his side of the lobby. I was relieved to see the man leave. I had the scary feeling that Mrs. Phillips thought Mike would back down on creating what would look like a fatal accident if she ordered my death, so she'd hired someone else to get rid of me in case she and I hadn't come to an agreement. And while she was at it, she'd take care of anyone else connected to the kidnapping.

Can this be true, or am I imagining things? Maybe I'm "seeing shadows" where there aren't any? Maybe the man was just being friendly? Somehow, I don't think that was the case.

I felt nervous as I sat down on the comfortable stuffed chair facing the plush sofa where Mike and Tom sat. Mike's face now had its usual coloring. Tom was beaming. I was in a state of shock. What had I done by agreeing to marry Tom? It was obvious that was who it was going to be, not Mike. I answered myself---I had agreed to stay alive, that's what.

"Looks like we have a weddin' tah plan," Mike said cheerfully. "I suggest the two of you elope tah the nearby state where there isn't the three day waitin' period."

Tom, sensing my unease, said to me gently, "We'll marry on any terms that suit you, Joan. We can stay married in name only for the year if that's what you want, but I'd like to share living in the same house with you. I presume you'll want to stay in your present home." I simply nodded. *Bless Tom. I'm finding more and more things to appreciate about him.*

Tom asked Mike if he would serve as the best man. Mike thought about that and decided he'd rather not have his name on the marriage document. "I'll be the weddin' photographer instead if'n you don't mind," he announced. Both Tom and I liked that idea.

Suddenly, my bracelet started vibrating. It was more than just a tingle. RUN, LEAVE, GO, it said. *What?* HURRY!

That doesn't make sense. NOW! came the words in the bracelet. Somehow, I was suddenly afraid. I jumped up and literally ran for the closest exit door.

"Joan!" exclaimed Mike. "What is it?" I didn't stop to reply. Tom came running after me. I reached the exit door, hurried down the steps and then wondered what to do.

HIDE, advised the bracelet.

Where? The only place to hide that I could see was behind the big bush next to the concrete porch of the hotel. I flew down the steps and pushed the branches aside. I tried to catch my breath once I was leaning against the building. Then I heard Tom who had followed me. "Joan, where are you?" he asked in desperate tones.

"Behind the bush," I answered. "Hurry down here."

Soon both Tom and I were huddled between the bush, the building and the corner of the hotel porch. "What's going on?" Tom whispered.

"Shhhhh," I motioned with my finger in front of my lips.

Some men came out of the hotel. Tom and I listened to their conversations. Several of them walked down the steps and went away, but two remained on the porch. "The club did a good thing electin' you president," said one voice. The other said, "Thank you."

I recognized that second voice. IT WAS RICHARD! I wanted to rise up and shout at him all in one breath, "Here I am, I love you, come save me." But I didn't. It would be like signing his death warrant. I was convinced Mrs. Phillips was very much in earnest regarding what she'd told me. If Claudia couldn't have Richard, then nobody else would.

The two men on the porch separated. As he walked away, I heard Richard humming the tune that had been his favorite ever since I'd met him. It was a lively melody, and I liked it too. He composed new words to it on the night he'd placed the engagement ring on my finger. We decided to call that tune Our Song. I doubted Richard was thinking of the new words to it as he walked towards wherever it was he'd parked his car. The new words to the song said, "There's a great day comin', When me and my darlin', Are together each twilight, And wake with arms entwined, Oh, happy weddin' day ahead." Memories flooded my mind.

As Richard walked away, I tried to hold back my sobs. My right fist ended up in my mouth. My forehead leaned against Tom's chest while my left fist kept hitting his right shoulder HARD. Tom just held me close. Finally, when I had my emotions under control, I pulled away from him. "I hope I didn't hurt you," I said sorrowfully. "That was Richard, and it was all I could do not to call out to him."

Just then, Mike on his crutches hobbled through the hotel door. He was carrying my purse. From our vantage point we could see him, but he didn't see us. Tom called out, "We'll join you in a minute. Come on down the steps."

Moments later, the three of us sat in Tom's car. "You must love him a lot tah know when he's close," Mike said after hearing the events of the last few minutes. I didn't say a word.   Mike smiled at me.   "This is still another proof that your word is tah be trusted, Joan. Musta been a mighty temptation tah call out tah him."

Tom added, "Here she is agreeing to marry me and loving him so much. Still, we'd better make plans for the wedding if you still want to go through with it, Joan." Both men looked at me expectantly.

What choice did I have if I didn't want to cause Richard's death? My own didn't seem to matter much at that point. I heaved a big sigh. "Yes, we'll continue with our plans," I said. "I gave Black Crow my word, and she promised not to harm Richard, me, Mike or Tom if I kept my total agreement with her. I have no doubt that Richard and I will both end up dead if I don't marry soon. I don't like it, but I don't see any way around it. I'm grateful to you, Tom, for agreeing to come to my rescue this way. I hope you don't end up getting emotionally hurt as a result."

"Yeah, Joan, I know there's that possibility, but I'm willing to chance it anyway." Tom tried to smile, but his expression turned out looking grim.

13

One thing led to another, and two days later, Mike, Tom and I were in the state where there was no waiting period for marriages. Mike rode with Tom and me in Tom's car. Mike paid for all the expenses en route including double rooms at the motel where we stopped overnight as well as the meals we ate plus the gasoline used in Tom's car for the trip. Mike said he was taking it out of the money Black Crow had paid him earlier. He also paid for the marriage license Tom and I secured at the County Courthouse. As we left the County Clerk's office, I said looking at Mike, "To set the record straight, my parole to you and Tom ends the moment I'm legally married. Is that right?"

"Yes, Cutie, I'll agree tah that. Once you 'n Tom are pronounced man 'n wife you'll no longer be under my control. What you 'n Tom work out between you is of no concern of mine." While Tom was in a telephone booth in the hall of the County Courthouse checking the telephone directory for something, Mike studied my face. He spoke softly.

"Obviously," Mike mused, "Tom is hopin' you'll fall in love with him before the year is up. 'N, who knows, maybe you will. He's a great guy, 'n Richard seems denied tah yah. I hope you know what you're doin' marryin' Tom."

Well, I did too, but I wasn't going to back out of the plans now. "Mike, I'll be able to take the official marriage document to my attorney soon. Then, I'll be assigned the sole trustee of the trust my mother has waiting for me and get to see what's in the brown envelope she instructed the attorney to hold for me until then. I think you'll be interested in the contents. Would you like me to have photocopies made for you if it shows Pete is my real father? I'm pretty sure that's what Mom will say in the envelope."

Mike didn't have a chance to answer because Tom came back saying excitedly that there was a jewelry store close. He wanted to buy a set of wedding rings. He hadn't thought of that before. He asked if I'd prefer gold or silver.

I decided I'd choose whichever was less expensive, but I replied, "Let's check out both and then decide."

"Sounds reasonable," Tom smiled. "We can do that. Well, that'll take care of the rings. What about the ceremony? Do you want it performed by a minister, priest, rabbi or what?" Tom was looking at me with adoration in his eyes. "If we have a religious service, we'll have to decide which kind."

"I had assumed we'd be married by a judge or some civil authority," I said hastily. "I'd rather not have a religious service until I take my wedding vows seriously." I think I hurt his feelings when I said that.

"I suppose a justice of the peace would do. What do you think, Mike?" Tom asked as if hoping Mike wouldn't agree with me.

Mike replied, "I think it's customary for the bride tah make the choice."

We inquired while still at the County Courthouse about seeing a judge to perform the ceremony. The helpful clerk at the information desk, after checking her records, said the two judges who might be available were both hearing court cases just then. She suggested—and I'm sure she thought it was to a pair of sweethearts she was anxious to help—that we could talk to the minister whose church was just four city blocks away. She even offered to get him on the phone for us. Mike took control and asked her to make the call. He talked with the minister and made arrangements for us to meet him at the church in an hour. The pastor asked if we'd like him to supply the two needed witnesses, and Mike said it would be appreciated. I was dreading what was coming. I truly didn't want a religious service for this particular wedding, but as it turned out I didn't have a choice. I was mindful that Richard and I were in danger until the ceremony was completed. I would still need to send an announcement to the Seymours, but first the ceremony had to take place. Might as well get it over with, I decided.

Tom drove to the jewelry store. While Tom and I went inside, Mike stayed in the car. When we left the store, there was a matching set of gold rings in Tom's pocket that he'd ended up selecting. Mike asked Tom to stop the car when we passed a florist shop. Tom and I waited while Mike hobbled on crutches inside the shop. He returned with a corsage of white and pink roses. I guess he remembered when I had said days ago that roses were my favorite flowers. He gave Tom a white rose to wear for the ceremony. We then had the marriage license, the wedding rings, and the wedding flowers.

I soon found myself standing with Tom before a minister inside a church with beautiful stained glass windows. The organ was to be played by the minister's wife. Two women who were strangers to me stood nearby as witnesses. Mike was taking pictures with Natalie's camera. *I wish I was standing here with Richard.* My heart was breaking and seemed to be crying, but I managed a weak smile at Reverend Joseph Melvin. He nodded his head towards his wife and beautiful organ music flowed through the church. I felt numb.

"Dearly beloved," started Rev. Melvin when the music stopped. I refused to listen to the rest of what he had to say until Tom nudged me with his elbow. Rev. Melvin was asking me if I would take this man, Thomas William Jensen, to be my lawfully wedded husband. I felt something like sand in my throat as I said, "Yes, I do." Tom gave me a big smile that Mike caught on film.

"Do you wish to make personal promises to each other at this special time?" asked Rev Melvin a bit later.

Tom turned towards me and reached for both of my hands. Holding them, he looked into my eyes and said earnestly, "I promise you, Joan, that I will be faithful to you for as long as we are married. For as long as I live, I will protect you with my life if it is ever necessary."

Then, it was my turn to make a wedding day pledge to my new husband. What to say? I ended up making a solemn statement, "I promise you, Tom, that I will be faithful to you for as long as we are married. I will do my best not to dishonor the last name you are bestowing upon me."

I think the minister had expected perhaps something different, but he went on to the double ring part of the ceremony. In the meantime, Mike was taking lots of pictures while moving around on his crutches. Finally, Rev. Melvin came to the part that was important. He pronounced Tom and I were husband and wife.

And then, he did what ministers do. He offered a prayer on our behalf. I thought it would never end! Mrs. Melvin played a lively tune as Tom kissed me after the minister said Tom could kiss his bride. Tom's kiss was full of passion and pent up emotion. His enthusiastic kiss startled me. I found myself kissing him back. Maybe it was sheer relief that the ceremony was finally over? Mike shook Tom's hand. I couldn't wait to get out of the church, but I was delayed doing that until the official papers were signed.

Mike stayed behind in the church as Tom and I waited in the car. I learned later that Mike had paid the minister for the service as well as giving something to the witnesses and Mrs. Melvin, but he didn't tell Tom and me how much. I didn't know until Mike mentioned it that the person performing the marriage ritual was the usual person to register the marriage and pay the fees involved. Mike told Tom and me that he had made arrangements for Rev. Melvin to immediately file the wedding document at the County Courthouse so it would be legally registered right away. He asked the minister to obtain three certified copies as soon as possible which would be proof that a legal marriage had taken place. Mike paid him amply for the extra trouble and fees. Mike told Rev. Melvin that he'd phone in about three hours to find out if the certified copies were available. If they were, Mike would make a donation to the church when he picked up the official documents. The money from Black Crow was being spread over a wide area.

"Nice weddin' service," Mike said when he joined us in the car.

"Yes, I think so too," Tom replied smiling.

I remained silent. I was thinking that a married woman didn't have to testify against her husband. While we were married, without my testimony, there would be no legal case against Tom should my kidnapping ever come to trial. With my description of the bearded man who captured me, Mike should be safe too. These two men had tried their best to keep me safe from Black Crow. They wouldn't deserve to be sentenced for kidnapping. Probably, there would never be a court hearing since my kidnapping was known only to those involved. My marriage, on the other hand, would be public knowledge. Well, I'd never have to be ashamed of the title of Mrs. Thomas Jensen. He was a fine man. Mrs. Joan Jensen. It would take time for me to become accustomed to being called that.

Our next stop was in a fast service photographic shop. Mike was told his pictures would be ready in about an hour and a half rather than the usual one hour service since he was ordering so many.

While we waited, we sat in a cafeteria near Main Street and ate apple pie topped with vanilla ice cream. Mike looked around and made sure no one except Tom would overhear us. Then he said to me, "One detail about what you've promised about not identifyin' me with your kidnappin' or anythin' regardin' it needs tah be cleared up. It occurs tah me that this so-called amnesia includes tahday. I give you permission tah talk about the weddin', but nothin' tah identify me. You might also find it convenient tah be able tah say that when you broke up with Richard, you stayed with the Jensens. I give you permission to say that as long as Tom approves which I believe he will. You are not, however, released from your oath regardin' me or anythin' else about your kidnappin' that you've promised tah keep secret. Understood?"

I looked at Mike steadily. "I agree not only to the words, but also to the spirit of what you are saying. I won't break your trust." I waited for Mike to ask for the Unicorn's sign or something, but he didn't. He simply nodded his head in acknowledgement of what I'd said.

Later that day in Cathy's Coffee Shop several blocks from where we'd had our apple pie earlier, I was given two copies of the certified marriage document and a bag of negatives along with pictures of the wedding. I noted that Mike wore gloves as he handled the items. He kept a set of the pictures and one copy of the certified marriage certificate. While Tom visited the men's room, Mike told me that Tom had refused all payment offered for his part in helping with the kidnapping. "I want tah give him a thank you for all his help," Mike added. "Please give him this envelope after I'm gone. Call it a weddin' gift. That'll make him feel free tah accept it." I slipped the envelope into my purse as Tom headed our way.

Tom sat down and turned towards Mike. "I've been thinking," he said. "According to what you told me, you and Natalie are going to get married right away 'n the two of you are going to move far away and change your names. If you do this, do you think it would matter if years from now, Joan was released from her promise of secrecy about the kidnapping, the why of her marriage to me, and the whole story without revealing who you are? What about once Joan has a grandchild who is nineteen years old like she is now, would she be permitted to tell the story? That'd probably be forty years or so from now. I'd give her my permission to tell my part of all of this then if you will agree allow her to talk about it when her grandchild reaches age nineteen."

Mike shrugged. "Forty years or so, huh? Nobody would be able tah find me by then. Sure, Cutie, I release you from your promise of secrecy providin' you don't reveal my current identity other than my first name when you have a grandchild who is nineteen like you are now. Agreed?

"I understand, Mike. I accept your limitation. Thank you." I smiled at him and then looked at Tom.

"Yes, I release you to talk about the affair then too, but you may use my name in the telling only if I'm not alive at the time." Tom smiled at me and then continued, "Hopefully, you see, we'll still be married by then if I have my way. Well, you might say you needed to marry, and I offered to be your husband to prevent you marrying someone else 'cause even then I was in love with you."

Mike interrupted. "I'm goin' tah leave the two of you here. I'll phone Natalie tah meet me after you go tah your hotel. She has already registered at a motel on the edge of town. You have reservations paid for in advance as Tom knows for tahnight. I don't care if'n you use one or two of the beds in the room, but it might be important that you can swear later that you spent your weddin' night in the same hotel room. Even git some folders about the hotel to take home with you."

Because it was so important to me, even though I'd asked before the wedding ceremony, I double checked. "Both of you agree that I am not under parole to either of you now that I'm married, right?" I looked first at Mike, and then stared at Tom. Being married to him was one thing, but needing to obey his orders and to always necessarily be truthful all the time was something else. Not that I expected to lie to him, but I wanted the freedom to act naturally. I turned back towards Mike when he spoke.

Mike was looking at me with a serious expression on his face. "Yes, Cutie, your parole tah me is no longer in force. For my peace of mind, I need you tah verify that your promise tah never reveal my last name is forever. I know you must have seen it on the boat registration while you were on the *Lucky*. When you have a nineteen year old grandchild, only then are you released from your promise of secrecy regardin' all of the rest. Do we each have this same understandin'?"

I understood how Mike felt. I'd felt the same way about wanting to be certain my parole to both him and Tom had come to an end. I raised my right hand, made the proper hand sign, and said, "Mike, I swear on my honor as a member of the Unicorn Organization that if a legal authority ever questions me about this kidnapping, I will describe my captor as the bearded man written about in my notebook. Until I have a grandchild who has reached the age of nineteen years, I will never reveal anything else to anyone about my kidnapping except for what happened today and the fact that I spent time in the Jensen home before my marriage.   I will never ever tell anyone your current last name. In no way will I knowingly do anything that would harm you—ever." I lowered my hand and then looked at Mike with tears in my eyes. "I owe you my life, Mike. I will never betray you." Mike nodded. I could tell that he believed me. He felt at ease now where I was concerned.

Then I turned towards Tom. It was important to me that he acknowledge that I was free of the obligations of behavior I had assumed as his prisoner.

"Yeah, Joan, you are no longer under parole to me," he said calmly, "but you are legally my wife, and I feel a responsibility for your well-being. Please allow me that privilege while you are Mrs. Thomas Jensen."

I felt a huge emotional load lift from my shoulders. I was free, Free, FREE and no longer anyone's prisoner. *Yippee! Oh, but I'm Tom's wife at least in the legal sense. Not quite totally free after all. Yes, but I no longer have to fear Black Crow. Somehow, I know that Tom and Mike have an agreement with each other about keeping the secrets of the involvement of each of them in the kidnapping affair.*

Tom said he wanted to call his mother and tell her our plans. She'd known we were eloping, but he wanted to fill her in on when we'd be returning. While Tom was doing that, I made sure no one was close enough to see me when I reached into my big purse and pulled out a plain brown paper bag containing Mike's gun, its holster with body harness, and the box of extra cartridges. "Thanks, Mike, for the loan of these. Having the protection was a good thing, but I won't need it now. Please take them back." I smiled. "I'd really feel relieved if you kept them."

Mike grinned and shook his head. "Keep 'em as a reminder of my good wishes, but check intah obtainin' a concealed weapons permit if'n you plan tah wear the gun hidden."

"Thanks," I said while replacing the still filled brown bag in my purse. "And before something else comes up, like it usually does when I've started to ask, what about your leg? After it was X-rayed, did you have to have it reset? Is it still painful?"

"You did a great job, Cutie. The doctor said it was fine jest as it was, but I did need a cast. He also said the pain would lessen over time, but it would take awhile."

I felt a huge sense of relief. I'd worried about his leg and if I'd done the right things, or made matters worse. Then I ventured another question that had been bothering me. "Have you learned how much damage there is to your boat?"

I was pleased to see Mike's smile even before he told me the good news. "The insurance claims adjuster told me that my boat can be repaired. The rear canvas is gone. Thar's a little damage on the ledges where the canvas was fastened. 'N there's a lot of smoke residue on top of the boat, but it isn't permanent. Since my boat has an inboard motor 'n recessed gasoline tank, it didn't suffer nearly as badly as some of the wood crafts that have outboard engines with exposed gas lines, tanks, 'n on some boats, filled gasoline cans on their decks. The Fiberglas hull on my boat helped too. After a small de-ductible, the insurance will cover all the necessary repairs tah the *Lucky.*"

Yes, Mike's boat has the correct name—Lucky. I felt relieved and happy for Mike. "I intended to return your boat door key the day we talked on the telephone with Black Crow. Somehow with all that was going on that day, I forgot." Reaching into my purse, I located the key and handed it to him. "You have a beautiful boat. I felt honored that you let me stay there. And while we have a little private time to talk, what do you intend to do about being my uncle? We both seem convinced that you are." I held my breath waiting for his reply.

"Yes, I feel sure you are Pete's daughter. I've been wantin' tah tell you that Pete 'n I had the same mother, but different fathers. My dad wanted tah adopt Pete, but when Pete found out he'd have tah change his last name in the process, he decided he liked the shorter last name he already had better. It was Hopkins. Peter Andrew Hopkins. He asked if'n he could call my father Dad anyway. 'N that's the way it ended. Dad had an allergy tah cats 'n dogs. Pete was disappoint-ed when he wanted a puppy 'n couldn't have one. He said when he had a kid, one of the first gifts on a fifth birthday would be a puppy named Woofer. That's what he had named his pretend dog."

"The more I hear about Pete, the nicer he sounds. Not that the father I knew wasn't great though." I sighed. "Mike, what about you and me?"

"I'm sorry, Joan. Maybe later we cin follow through on it. I suppose you'll keep your current house. I can always write tah yah thar. Somehow, I'd let you know it was me without actually sayin' so. I'm afraid of Black Crow 'n what she might take intah her head tah do tah git rid of me for some reason her mixed up mind might think was important tah her safety. I don't trust her one bit. I'm surprised that you trust her promise." Mike shook his head. "That's one mixed up character!"

"Since I know who she is and what she was after, and some of her background—like what would be a sacred oath to her—it's easier for me to trust her word. I'm not afraid of what she'd do to us as long as I keep my promises to her. And I fully intend to do that. I don't think you and Natalie are in danger from her, but I understand how you feel." *I do trust what Black Crow—Mrs. Phillips— promised me BECAUSE the messaging bracelet told me she'd live up to her word.*

"Actually, there's someone else I'm in trouble with 'n he frightens me even more than Black Crow does. I've been told I'm tah be a reluctant key witness against him in a trial scheduled next month. Dealin' with shady characters as I sometimes do in my business has its drawbacks. I want tah retire from this kind of life 'n live a more wholesome one---raise chickens or cattle---or do something else instead. Natalie 'n I will get married this week. It will be in a different city than this though. I don't want Black Crow tah check the records here for your marriage 'n find mine as well. Natalie 'n I were goin' get married the end of December anyway. It's convenient tah do it now." Mike's smile lit up his whole face. "Natalie is all for the idea. Elopin' instead of havin' a big weddin' doesn't bother her."

"Mike, I've been wondering something. Would you really have created a fatal so-called accident for me if Black Crow ordered it?"

He looked at me briefly before replying. "When I agreed tah do it if'n I couldn't convince you tah do what she wanted, I was sure it would never become an issue. I was scared it would when you refused her order tah marry me. I knew then that I jest couldn't do it. I was afraid Natalie would be in danger unless I figured a way tah hide her. I was so relieved when you settled the issue with Black Crow tah her satisfaction." Mike gave me a brilliant smile. I felt good knowing my trust in Mike was vindicated. *I bet Mrs. Phillips suspected Mike couldn't commit murder, and she had the standby waiting in the hotel lobby watching us and waiting for the order to complete that task or walk away if his services weren't needed. I may be wrong, but I doubt it.*

Mike went on to say, "I have a confession tah make. I figured you were so frightened of black spiders that I could fool you intah believin' my Halloween plastic one was real. I was careful not tah let you get a good look at it. I know you felt threatened by it, but you did promise tah write the necessary letter tah Richard. It was ever so important that you do that." Mike laughed, and so did I after a moment.

Wanting to be certain Mike could contact me later, I told him, "I'm going to change my telephone number to an unlisted one under Tom's initials and last name. I'll get a post office box so if you ever want to contact me, you can. I'll burn your correspondence as soon as I can after reading it. I'll leave a message on your office answering machine if you aren't back yet from your honeymoon. I'll say something like, 'The ticket number you want is…..' You'd know that would mean my post office box is that number. You might want to give me your office telephone number since you won't be using it much longer. I'll call from a pay phone in case anyone is tracing your calls. I'll change my phones too in case somehow my two phones have a hidden tracing or recording device. Someone might have sneaked in to install those. I really want a way for you and me to stay in touch, Mike, if later you want to do that. Would you want me to tell Tom if you do correspond with me, or is it to be just yours and my secret unless you tell me differently?"

Mike thought about it before he replied. "Do you have paper 'n a pen I can use?" I did and handed them to him. "Here is the office phone number, but add one digit tah each number. For example, a three would actually mean four." Mike smiled when he handed the sheet of paper and pen back to me. "I trust you completely, Joan, or I wouldn't even consider your suggestion. For the time bein', don't tell even Tom about our arrangement—or anyone else." I nodded. He knew I'd keep the secret if I did that.

"I'll include my new unlisted telephone number in my message to your office," I added thoughtfully. "I'll do like you did with your telephone number—you'll need to add one digit to each number. Do this for this for my post office box number too. I'll say it is Margaret calling with the information you requested."

Mike smiled. "On second thought, Cutie, when you have a grandchild who is as old as you are now, you cin say that I'm your uncle without mentionin' my current last name, but never reveal more about me after tahday unless sometime in the future I tell you differently or you feel intuitively that I would approve. I trust you enough tah know you'd be careful about what you tell others about me. If'n it seems safe tah me, I'll try tah contact you around Christmas each year at least."

"I agree. Thanks, Uncle Mike." My eyes were shinning with tears. This new arrangement meant a lot to me. I felt certain the contents of my mother's brown envelope would confirm that Pete was my father and that would verify that Mike was indeed my uncle.

I had been watching Tom and noticed when he left the telephone booth and headed our way. Mike and I were lucky we had so much time for our private conversation.

Tom said his sister, Mary, was visiting their mother, and she wanted to chat a bit. She was pleased to hear about his marriage and was looking forward to meeting her new sister-in-law.

My heart was overflowing when I hugged Mike. "You saved my life. I owe you so much. You were right to believe Black Crow was a real threat. After she talked with me, I realized how serious she was about ordering my death if I didn't cooperate with her demands. You were certainly correct about that! You went out of your way to protect me. I know it involved more to you than being just another job. I can never thank you enough."

Tom added, "I deeply appreciate what you did too and for including me in trying to save Joan's life. I realize it was a huge gamble on your part. Thanks for trusting me and for saving her." Tom gave Mike a heartfelt hug.

After all we'd been through together, it was hard to finally tell Mike goodbye when Tom and I started to leave the coffee shop. We realized he would phone Natalie, and she would come to pick him up. We also felt that he was protecting Natalie by avoiding our meeting her. As we started to go out the door, I turned back and hugged Mike again with tears in my eyes. I owed him my life, and words seemed so inadequate to express my gratitude. I was glad he was my uncle even if it was a secret between us.

■ ■ ■

Late the next evening, Tom and I returned to the apartment where his mother lived. Mrs. Jensen met us with a wide smile. She took me in her arms and said, "Welcome to the family, dear Joan. I'm glad to accept ye as my new daughter. Tom seems so happy. Thank ye for that." She gave me a heartfelt kiss on my check. I turned and hugged her. "Thank you," I told her. How different she was from Mrs. Seymour. Her reaction was vastly nicer than I would have had from Richard's mother had he and I eloped. I felt tears in my eyes.

I pretended a headache after supper, and Tom suggested to his mother that they allow me to go to bed while the two of them sat up and talked. Once in bed, I felt my right wrist as I had often done these last few days, but not yesterday or last night as I had a lot of other things on my mind then. Touching the bracelet had become sort of a ritual to me, especially before I fell asleep. I didn't feel the message bracelet this time. I turned on the light and saw it was missing. I was surprised to realize how much I had learned to count on it to give me information I needed. I was going to miss it, but I remembered Smoke Man had told me when it would disappear. I felt so lucky to have had it when I needed it most. I sent a thought message of thanks to Smoke Man. I knew I didn't need to speak aloud to him. Then I sent a very sincerely felt prayer of thanksgiving to the Almighty for the help and protection I'd been given through Smoke Man. I knew he'd been sent in answer to my desperate prayer aboard Mike's boat.

When Tom came later to join me in his bedroom, I pretended to be asleep. He quietly removed a sleeping bag from the closet and rolled it out on the floor beside the double bed. He had carefully locked the bedroom door. His mother would have been surprised if she had known our sleeping arrangements for that night.

14

Somehow, after all he'd done to try to help me, I couldn't bring myself to refuse Tom's request to share my house. He agreed that we'd each have our own bedroom. Tom suggested that he change the locks on all the outside doors and that we wouldn't give anyone a spare key at the present time. I agreed. He also took care of installing new telephones in the hall and in the master bedroom. Those were the only two telephones in the house. (Many homes in those days had only one telephone. It was generally either in the hall or on a kitchen wall.) I suggested Tom use the master bedroom with its attached bathroom. I preferred to keep the same bedroom that I'd had for years. I could continue to use the hall bathroom.

At the first opportunity, I had my telephone number changed to an unlisted number under Tom's name using his initials. I also obtained a post office box. When I telephoned Mike's office, I was transferred to its answering machine. I left the message I'd told Mike I would. I added that the brown envelope we had talked about confirmed the information we were expecting. It was my way of telling him he was indeed my uncle.

Tom and I moved to my house the day after we stayed overnight at the Jensen apartment. The first afternoon I was home, I used a special pen and India ink to calligraphy on a sheet of parchment paper the announcement of my marriage with the date, place, and names of the bride and groom. I even drew a rose in the top left hand corner. I thought the final result of the wedding announcement looked professional. I enclosed a snapshot that Mike had taken of Tom and me just after we'd been pronounced man and wife. I felt like crying, but I did as necessary to notify the Seymours of my marriage. I took the envelope addressed to Richard Seymour and Parents to the post office where I dropped it in the out-going mail slot. I hoped all this would satisfy Mrs. Phillips. I was doing what I'd promised her. That was important so she'd keep her word to me.

After I'd been home three days, I decided to call Aunt Sarah. I knew I would be in for a tongue lashing and had made excuses to myself for not calling her sooner. Still, she needed to know the latest news.

"Hello, Aunt Sarah," I said cheerfully when she answered my call.

"Oh, you finally decided to get in touch with me," she snarled. "No call at Thanksgiving and no way to call you. And you even forgot to call me on my birthday." She was getting more upset with each word she uttered. "I don't know why you even bothered to call me now. Richard called me three times asking about you. I wasn't able to tell him anything about where you were except on a trip with a girl from college. What were you thinking when you broke your engagement? The man loves you. Now you won't be getting any of that family's wealth. SHAME ON YOU!"

"But don't you care about what I feel? Doesn't what I want count for any-thing? Was the money involved with my possible connection to the Seymours your most important consideration?"

"Well, you have to admit, money is important," sputtered Aunt Sarah. "And how come I wasn't important enough for you to call on my birthday. How could you forget?"

"Auntie, I would have called you if I could. Did it ever occur to you that I might have been in an accident and in the hospital for days? Don't you even care about me, but only about yourself?" I'd never thought of her this way before. I was so upset that I said, "'Bye." I slammed the telephone handset into its cradle and stomped into the kitchen. I hadn't told her I was married nor given her my new telephone number. I wondered if she'd try to call me back. If she did, she'd get the recording saying that the number was no longer in service, and no forwarding one was listed.

I was so upset that I went to the freezer and took out a package of vanilla ice cream. That was my favorite comfort food. I hadn't intended to keep spooning it out and was surprised how much was in my bowl. I put half of it back into the carton. Once that was back in the freezer, I sat down at the table to slowly let the cold stuff melt in my mouth as I fumed emotionally. I was halfway through the ice cream in the bowl when I decided to get some chocolate cookies to go with it. Once all this was in my stomach, I felt a bit better. (A few years later when I started gaining weight, I stopped eating so many of my comfort foods and found other ways to deal with stress.) I was very disappointed with Aunt Sarah, but she was entitled to her own opinions. I just didn't have to agree with her nor continue to keep in close contact with her either. I'd let time take care of my dealings with her.

Suddenly, it occurred to me that I was being guilty of just what I'd accused her of being. That is, thinking of only herself and not caring about my feelings. Here I was feeling hurt and not thinking about how worried she probably had been about my not calling for so long, and especially not on her birthday when I'd made it a habit to always do that. She likely waited for the call that never came. I went to the hall phone and dialed her number.

"Aunt Sarah," I said, "I understand about your being worried about me when I didn't call for so long. Truly, I did think about it, but circumstances were such that I couldn't. Are you all right? Have you been sick or anything?"

This time she and I had a nice conversation. She had been worried about me. It was so unlike me not to call on her birthday, she said, that she was afraid I'd died or something. Finally, I worked up my courage to tell her of my marriage to Tom. She had a hard time digesting that. Somehow, while we talked about my marriage, I forgot to give her my new telephone number. I felt I needed to tell her I was married and, knowing her, I figured she'd call Richard once I hung up the phone. This would confirm the announcement I'd already sent to the Seymours. So far, they hadn't bothered to send any congratulations, but it was really too soon to expect any. I was hoping they'd neglect responding. It would be easier for me that way. If Richard tried to phone me, he'd get the no longer in service message.

Mrs. Connor had been away when I first arrived home. She was back, I noticed, the evening after I'd talked with Aunt Sarah. When I went next door to see her, Mrs. Connor hugged me in a very emotional way. When she learned I'd married the man who had been taking care of my place while I was away, she was simply delighted. "Tom seems like a fine person," Mrs. Connor said. "You have a lot more in common with him than you do with Richard. I guess you figured that out for yourself. Besides, now maybe you'll continue living next door. If you'd married Richard, I was afraid you'd move away, and we'd not see much of each other. Incidentally, Richard stopped in to ask me about you several times. I didn't have any more information to give him.

The last I'd heard, you were on a trip with your college girl friend. It was smart of you to make it so I could truthfully say I didn't know anything new. I would have hated to lie about it if you didn't want him to know where you were. You know me well enough to have figured that out. I appreciate your thoughtfulness."

How different from Aunt Sarah's reaction, I thought.

The day after Christmas, a neighbor boy wearing a Boy Scout uniform knocked on my front door. We knew each other, so I said, "Hello, Johnny. How's things going for you?"

"A man I never saw before gave me five dollars to bring you something," Johnny told me. "He said if you didn't want to keep it, I was to find a different home for it or take it to the pound."

"Well, where is it?" I didn't see a package or anything.

Johnny went back through the front gate and brought a large basket that he'd left on the sidewalk. Then he set it down in front of me and removed the lid. Inside was an adorable puppy who raised his head and stared at me.

"What breed is it? What else did the man say? Did he give you any hint of the occasion or the reason for the gift?" I was puzzled.

"The man said you'd know who sent the puppy when you look at the name tag. The dog comes from a litter of a neighbor of his. The mother dog is a gentle German shepherd. The sire of the puppy is unknown, the man said. Do you want to keep the puppy, or can I have him?" Johnny looked eager.

I looked at the name tag on the puppy's collar. It said WOOFER. I knew this gift was Mike's way of acknowledging that I was Pete's daughter, and that he was giving me what he knew his brother would have wanted me to have. In no way did I want to give the little dog away! Also in the basket was a dog leash, a doggie feeding dish and some puppy dog food. Woofer laid his head back on the basket's pillow. He kept his eyes glued on me.

"Thanks, Johnny. I'll keep little Woofer. Would you like to bring the basket into the house for me and also meet my new husband?" Johnny left after having a big bowl of vanilla ice cream and a large handful of chocolate cookies. He petted Woofer and was smiling when he went home.

Tom wondered who would send us a puppy.

"Maybe it's Mike's way of telling us he got back home okay. He told me his brother had a pretend dog named Woofer. He knew I'd remember the name and then know who sent the puppy. Isn't the little fellow cute? Do you mind if we keep it, Tom? You don't have an allergy to dogs, do you?"

Tom looked at me cuddling Woofer. "No, honey, I don't mind if you want to keep him. He'll probably keep us up a few nights in the beginning though." Tom was smiling as he watched me.

Two days later when I went to the post office to check my box there, I found an envelope containing Woofer's puppy shots record. There wasn't any note in the envelope, but now I was certain that Mike had received my telephone answering machine message.

I did return to college. It seemed to me that I had been gone for months, but actually it was only about four weeks and part of that time included the university's mini-vacation for Thanksgiving. I'd kept up on my homework, thanks to Tom's getting me the assignments. I'd even completed two term papers while I was away from classes. I'd written them in my extra thick typewriter paper size spiral notebook and turned them in when I returned to classes. (In those days, longhand term papers were acceptable although typed ones were much preferred.) I felt lucky that my professors accepted my absences with the excuse Tom had given them, and I was allowed to continue my classes. It was too late to drop a class without receiving a failing grade unless I took a special examination—and those would require an extra fee for each class. It was fortunate that I was able to continue with my classes in spite of the many days I'd been absent. I hadn't expected to be able to do that. The semester's final examinations were hard, but I'd studied well and passed the tests with good grades. I signed up for courses for the next semester. Tom kept his job, went to college classes, and was careful to keep his distance from me. Even though he had missed classes this current semester, he finished all them with good grades. He signed up for more classes for the next semester. I started feeling comfortable with him in the house.

After I'd been legally married for three months, I read in the newspaper about Richard's marriage to Claudia. My heart cried out in protest, but at least he and I were both still alive.

Six months rolled by. I found myself caring more and more about Tom. No, not the passionate in-love emotion I still felt about Richard but a comfortable solid feeling. Eventually, my feelings deepened, and I realized I loved Tom in a much different way than I did for Richard. I knew there was no hope for Richard and me. Gradually, I had started thinking of Tom as a partner and how I'd miss him if he moved somewhere else.

When I got up enough courage to mention how my feelings towards him had matured into something I felt was solid and lasting, Tom asked me if there was any hope that I'd accept him as a husband. When I answered yes, Tom was overjoyed. We ended up having a private ceremony all by ourselves beneath a full moon. He placed what to most people would look like an engagement ring next to my wedding band. After that, we shared the master bedroom. In due time, we had three children, Judy Alice, James Michael, and Janet Rose. My life seemed full, and I was happy.

We invited "Mom" Jensen to come live with us. She said she was honored we'd ask, but she preferred to stay in her own place unless she became unable to take care of herself. We did visit often. I came to love her dearly.

I earned my Associate of Arts degree, but then stopped going to university classes when I became pregnant with our first child. Tom became a successful licensed physical therapist and enjoyed his profession. I liked being able to be a stay-at-home mom.

About five years after Tom and I were established as a happily married couple, there was a big headline in our local newspaper announcing that the Unicorn Organization had been classified as a cult by some legal investigating committee. The article said the organization had practiced mind control over its members in a very subtle, but effective way. I thought back to when I had first heard of the organization as a child. It was known as a benevolent association that did a lot of good. I remembered when Susan, my friend who felt sorry for me after the loss of my immediate family, suggested I go with her to a party the Unicorn Organization was giving to celebrate its twenty-fifth anniversary. Susan thought it would be good for me to have a happy evening. One thing led to another, and I started going with her to several sponsored events the organization provided. I enjoyed meeting new friends there. When I was invited to formally become a member, I felt honored and accepted. Members were encouraged to attend meetings every two weeks. I learned that I'd been accepted into a preliminary trial membership. There would be more advantages to being initiated into full membership. In that initiation, I accepted obligations that I would never have thought of doing earlier. One thing led another as time went by. Gradually, the organization suggested things that I somehow felt as being right. Being able to take an oath that Mrs. Phillips accepted as being binding was probably a good thing. Looking back on it, why didn't I feel free to call the police when I discovered who Black Crow was? It was because then I was convinced it was totally imperative to keep my Unicorn Organization member's oath. Yes, I'd been brainwashed into believing that and other things. The more I thought about it, the more convinced I was that I'd been a fool. I withdrew my membership from the organization, but I still felt bound by the oaths I'd made as one of its members. The promises I made then had been sacred to me at the time and still were.

Tom's mother died shortly before the birth of our youngest child. I missed "Mom" Jensen a lot. A bit later, I heard on a television newscast of the passing of Mrs. Serena Seymour. Mrs. Martha Phillips died years later. Aunt Sarah lived to be an old woman. Mr. Byron Seymour and his son, Richard, played in golf tournaments, and I saw newspaper accounts of them doing other things together over the years. Eventually, Richard's father was placed in a nursing home and later died there. I saw his obituary in the local newspaper.

One Saturday afternoon after coming back from a shopping trip, Tom noticed smoke coming out of an upper widow of an apartment complex. Concerned, he parked his car and stood on the sidewalk. Beneath the smoke of an open window, two children were leaning out and crying for help. When Tom yelled up to ask where their parents were, the oldest boy replied that Mommy went to the store and Daddy was working. Tom asked what apartment they were in, and without thinking it through, he dashed into the building to rescue the children. He hadn't thought about providing himself with any protection from smoke. As he passed through the smoke-filled first floor hall, he pounded on doors shouting, "FIRE!" The stairs heading to the upper floor apartments were filled with smoke and so was the upper floor hallway. Tom was coughing hard by the time he reached the door of the apartment with the children. He knocked and then knocked even harder on that door. Finally, it opened. He went into the apartment and removed the coverings of two pillows. He placed one over each child's head to help prevent smoke damage to their lungs. He couldn't do that for himself because he needed to see where he was going. He carried one child under each arm. The smoke was worse on his exit route. Tom had problems seeing through it when he tried getting to the main front door. He kept coughing harder and harder. It was difficult to breathe. The smoke was dense and felt like

it was burning his lungs. Once outside, he handed the two children to a specta-
tor and then collapsed onto the sidewalk. An ambulance took him to the emergency room in the nearest hospital. He ended up with serious smoke inhalation
problems that caused his death a day later. He and I had been married just over
twenty-three years when he died. I saved the long article in our local newspaper telling about what a hero Tom had been and announcing his funeral. The
parents of the two children he saved sent a huge wreath with a banner saying
THANK YOU! I carefully saved the banner after the funeral.

A few days after Tom's final service, a newspaper article said that before the
fire, the owner had sold the old condemned ten apartment complex to a man
expecting to tear down the building and build a new one. All but three tenants
had already moved to other locations. These three were in the process of moving. The fire had apparently started when a man went to sleep while smoking
in bed. He was a night watchman. It was speculated that he had taken a double
dose of sleeping pills before lighting the cigarette. The other tenant who lived
downstairs was away at work when the fire started. The new owner decided to let
the building burn when he was notified of the problem by his friend who had a
business across the street. It took only five minutes for the apartment complex
owner to arrive at the scene. When he did, he asked the fire department to concentrate on protecting the adjacent buildings. It would have been too late to save
the burning apartment complex anyway. Two fire department trucks arrived after Tom and the children plus the night watchman were safely outside. Just after
the fire trucks parked, a huge crash came from inside the building. The floor
of the upper story had collapsed. Had Tom waited longer, the children could
have fallen through their apartment floor into the fiercely burning area below, a
newspaper article suggested. Perhaps some of the fire department crew would
have been hurt had they been in the building at the time when the burning upper
floor had dropped, the article speculated. The sleeping man was severely burned
when he finally awakened with pain. He looked dazed when he walked out of the
building just before the upper apartment floor collapsed. The apartment building was old with no overhead sprinklers. Once the fire had started, the building
was like kindling, the newspaper article quoted someone as saying.

Tom had the foresight to leave me a large insurance policy which I invested
wisely. Years passed. My children grew up and married. I stayed in the same house

my parents had left me. Time somehow moved on. I kept busy with this and that. I enjoyed being a part-time library assistant. I joined a couple of clubs. I sometimes babysat one set of grandchildren or another. I was as content as possible. I missed Tom dreadfully. I still felt a special spot in my heart for Richard. He seemed a part of me deep inside that was hard to describe and which seemed wise not to think about. Life moved on.

Mike's Christmas card with a note arrived each year in my post office box. I learned that he and his wife had new first and last names, but he didn't tell me what they were. They had two children as time went by. I could tell by the postage stamps that Mike was living in a different country, but I don't feel free to mention which one. There was never a return address on the envelopes. Mike phoned sometimes—months apart—to ask what was happening in my life. Woofer turned out to be a great dog, and Tom and I were glad to have him. Our children loved Woofer too.

About three years ago, I received a typed letter sent to my post office box address. It began by saying the writer had sad news to tell me. My uncle had passed away peacefully in his sleep. He'd often spoken of me, and he was pleased I was doing so well. His wife decided to stay where she was as their children had married locally, and her life was happy there. This would be the last correspondence I would receive from the writer, so I should feel free to dispense with my post office box if I wished. The letter was signed, "Curly's sister-in-law."

And yes, the contents of my mother's brown envelope did tell me Pete was my actual father and more details about what had happened. I learned that both my real parents had tried to act honorably after their one and only time of "getting carried away," and I respected them even more. Pete had gone to his base Chaplin and asked for help in keeping the name of the beneficiary confidential on his G.I. insurance. That's why Mike couldn't discover from it the name of the lady who Pete thought was having his child.

Mom said after a brief visit, her husband realized his mother-in-law was tired and needed a rest. He had thoughtfully gone with their son to his parents' home for the weekend to give Mom and her mother some quiet time together. That's why Mom was alone at the hospital. My mother had taken her wedding rings to the jewelry store to be resized and wasn't wearing them when Pete saw her. Mom explained several things that I'd wondered about.

Mom said she suspected who my father was the moment she first looked at me. Years later, she'd collected hair samples from the combs of both me and her husband. She'd taken them secretly for some kind of test. It proved we weren't blood related, but my legal father never knew and thought I was his. He always treated me like I was his special little girl—even when I was a teenager, and I liked it!

Mom had invested Pete's G.I. insurance funds and had doubled them over the years. I had access to them once I gave Mr. Williams, the attorney, a copy of the certified marriage document. I didn't need the funds at the time, so I left them in the Trust. I contacted the investment broker Mom had used, and the funds continued to grow over the years. I did need them later and was grateful they were available. In Mom's envelope was a picture of Pete. I still treasure it. He had sent it to Mom for her to save for the baby if it proved to be his as he expected it would. Mom had decided to tell me the truth about who my biological father was in case later on I needed to know family medical history. My legal father's liver and kidney problems would not be passed down to me from him. His failing eye sight need not concern me either. As far as she knew, Pete had good eyes, a strong heart and healthy lungs. He was a fine person, and I could be proud to be his daughter. She left it to my judgment about whether I'd want to tell the children I'd have someday about Pete, but please, she urged, not while your legal father is alive. It would hurt him immensely knowing about it, and he didn't deserve that.

Inside the brown envelope was the correspondence she'd saved from Pete. I read each page of it eagerly. I learned that Pete had written his parents that he was changing the beneficiary on his G.I. insurance to the mother of his child. He told them she'd contact them later if she wished. I did find their names listed in that particular letter along with a telephone number, but Mike had told me his parents had passed away by the time he and I met. Pete told his parents that the lady went by the nickname of Red. All of what was in Mom's brown envelope was fascinating to me. She mentioned that I'd been born three weeks earlier than the expected "due date." She wanted to mop the kitchen floor before special guests arrived. Apparently, she strained something in the process of working vigorously getting the task done fast. She ended up having labor pains and was rushed to the hospital.

I found it interesting that in a letter to my mother from Pete in the brown envelope, he said that after my mother left his motel room, Pete had gone to visit his friend, David, and to tell him goodbye as Pete would be leaving very early the next morning. When Pete got back to his room, he prayed hard that all would go well with her and then prayed about David who was suffering from a severe infection in his legs. If his high fever hadn't improved by the next morning, one of the options talked about was amputation of both legs. In the letter that David wrote later to Pete, it seemed a miracle had happened by the next morning. David's fever was gone! Pete and David did not have the same religious backgrounds, and that made the verse David sent Pete in his next letter all the more precious to Pete. Along with the verse came a note with an update about how much better David was feeling. Pete received the correspondence at his army station overseas. David in his note pointed out that God is known by various names depending much upon the society in which a person is born. For example, the American Indians had used the name *Great Spirit* when the first white settlers made contact with them.

David said when his spiritual help came, he was given to understand that it had come as a result of Pete's sincere prayer. David added that the awesome and inspiring healing contact with a powerful, wise and benevolent male personality spirit had been a life changing experience. It was interesting, he added, that a little while later a thought came as if it was from another spirit. It said the healing was temporary. David felt the healing had been complete and replied in positive tones, "I claim the healing." The doubting spirit tried, but couldn't change David's mind. It gave up and went away. David's note said the poetic meter might not be just right, but the verse he'd written was the best he could do in time to include it in that particular letter. He didn't know how else to best express what he felt. After reading those comments, I read a copy of David's verse.

A SONG OF THANKSGIVING

A song of thanksgiving
One of hope and gladness
For no longer do I feel alone
With thoughts so forlorn.

A prayer from a friend changed this
And the answer came swift,
A healing of body for sure
And of spirit as well.

Does it matter, really,
By what name He is known
In one culture or another
If God's help is always there?

Help might come by God's helper
And help me He really did.
I'm grateful that He would
And did it so completely.

A song of thanksgiving
This sings in my heart.
My spirit is much lighter and
Life seems a lot brighter.

May you too be blessed
When you sincerely ask in prayer
And receive the help you seek
Along with a feeling of serenity.

And when life gets hectic
With worries and stress,
Remember to pause and find peace
In this same glorious inner song.

I copied this verse onto parchment paper, framed it and hung it in my bedroom. At one time or another, each of my children individually asked who wrote the poem. I always answered that a friend of hers had given it to my mother, and she'd shared it with me.

I'd lived during a time as a child when cell phones and computers would have been something in comic strips, not real day-to-day "necessities." Microwaves in homes were unheard of when I was little, but I certainly enjoyed having one in my later life. I'd seen the advent of wide screen television as well as other modern day inventions. The idea of vehicles able to fly to planets even further from the earth than the moon would have been something to scoff at when I was in high school. I liked the improvements made in automobiles. My grandparents would have been amazed about such things as power steering, automatic transmission, buttons to operate opening and closing windows as well as adjusting the outside side mirrors, a way to wash the windshield with the movement of a lever and even the latest thing I heard about—a way to tell from the driver's seat when a tire's inflation has become low. Many things and ideas in the world had changed a lot over the years, but not the secret place in my heart that still remembered Richard. I've had a long interesting life. I'm grateful for my many blessings including good health, my marriage to Tom, our children and grandchildren. Yes, life has been good to me.

EPILOGUE

Clara Clark, Joan's nineteen year old granddaughter, wiped her fingers on a paper napkin after nibbling the last cookie from the plate in the middle of the kitchen table. "I had no idea you went through all of that, Grandma. I never guessed you had a boyfriend before Grandpa. You 'n him always seemed so happy together."

Joan smiled. "Our real marriage was happy," she admitted gladly. "I was lucky, so lucky, that he was patient with me until I accepted him as my husband. That was a good choice on my part. He was a loving partner and a fine father to our children."

"I wish I had a messaging bracelet to tell me what to do about me and Bob," sighed Clara.

"I hope you never get to the point where you feel the desperate need for help that I did when I prayed for it while on the boat. I've heard the saying, *God works in mysterious ways*. I sure believe it after Smoke Man and the bracelet experience. But, what about you and Bob? You seem to be saying that he is like two different people. The sober one is special, but the drinking one is not, at least in a good way. Can you cope with that?"

"Your story helps me see that even if Bob 'n I don't make up and get married, I'll still be all right. I can see that maybe Bob 'n me might not be good for each other—least not while we have this terrible difference standing between us. He doesn't want to quit drinking 'n I can foresee that could become a big problem between us--especially if it happened more and more often. What if he got more violent when he had too much to drink? Maybe like you did, you still loved Richard, but found you could love someone else in a different way. Maybe that could happen for me? Do you suppose?"

"Well, you know one of my favorite words is *options*. I guess you'll be able to figure out what yours are. It isn't like you have to decide right this minute what to do."

"Yeah, that's right," Clara muttered. "I do have time to think about it."

"My mother once told me that solving a problem comes in five parts. First, recognize what the problem is. Separate its parts if necessary. She titled this section *PROBLEM*. Second, gather information about the problem from knowledgeable sources. She called this *DATA*. Third, from the data collected, decide which steps are best to use in solving the problem. She named this step *OPTIONS*. Fourth, is having the patience and persistence to see the process though once the solution is decided upon. She called this part *PERSISTENCE*. Fifth, if there is no workable solution to the problem, a person has to decide whether to move from the environment of the problem—often hard to do—or to change one's reaction to the problem. In other words, adjust one's thoughts regarding it. She called this process *PERSPECTIVE*."

Clara leaned forward and listened attentively.

"As I grew older, I added two more steps to the process. One is *communication* if someone else is involved. And the other is *agreement* with that person about what the problem is, and what can be done about it. Like with you and Bob. His idea of what the problem is doesn't seem to coincide with yours. He may feel you are being unduly aggressive about it. That could put him on the defensive which makes him feel like arguing back. He may not understand the stress his drinking puts on you. You may not realize why he feels he wants to join his buddies for a series of social drinks. Apparently, he doesn't seem to feel he does it in excess. Well, I'm sure you'll figure out how you want to handle your problem."

Clara nodded, but said nothing.

"Actually," Joan added, "my mother said a number of things that helped me as I was growing up and afterwards too. One of her sayings, your mom's favorite, claims that a *"chicken"* does things just to prevent being called one. The really brave person doesn't give in to taunts and jeers from others when it goes contrary to held beliefs or personal safety. That's *true courage*. But, this is way off the subject. Do you think Bob will phone you when he gets over his angry spell?"

"Well, he just might. I sure hope he does. I'd like to discuss our problem further with him. 'N, like your mother said, maybe we can collect data about it, and then decide what our options are that would be satisfactory to each of us. Maybe he's right—the best one might be the one he said—just not get married. At least, the decision would come from figuring it out logically 'n not from a fit of anger. Actually now that I think about it, I believe a good subtitle under your word *agreement* would be *compromise*."

Joan nodded her head.

"Gee, Grandma, thanks for sharing your story 'n your mother's insights." Clara got up and hugged Joan. "Maybe you're right—broken engagements don't always have to stay broken. But, suddenly I'm realizing other things. I was thinking of the wedding, the excitement of it, but not too much about actually living day after day with Bob 'n the routine married life would bring. We'd need to work out some details about that. I do love him 'n would like to share my life with him. Maybe Bob and I can work out our problem. Oh, I'm so glad I came to talk with you!"

"I'm glad you came too, Clara," Joan replied smiling.

"If Bob doesn't call me in the next day or so, I'll phone him," stated Clara in a relieved tone. Obviously, she no longer felt things were completely out of her control. "I know now that if our engagement does have to end, I don't want it to happen in the bitter way it is now. Maybe there's a way to mend it. Somehow, though, I sense we're not going to be able to fix it."

Just then, the hall telephone rang. Joan answered it, and then passed the telephone on its long cord to Clara. "It's for you," she said.

"Bob?" asked Clara. Joan shrugged.

"Hello," practically sang Clara. She smiled thinking it was Bob. Then her expression changed to wonder. "Tony, is it really you?"

Joan remembered Tony Todd had been Clara's steady boyfriend when she a sophomore and junior in high school. They'd lost contact when he'd graduated a year ahead of her and enlisted in the army. He had been promised training in the field he wanted by the Army Recruiter. Tony decided that would be like getting paid to learn his vocation. It would be a lot less expensive than paying for college or vocational school tuition. Joan wondered how the army training had worked out for him. Had he realized the changes that would happen if he left civilian life? Had it seemed worth it to him? Once he was sworn it, it would have been too late to change his mind. Enlisting during peace time was so different than being "drafted" during times of war. Yet if there was a national emergency, the peace-time enlisted person might be right in the middle of coping with it. Well, it was Tony's life, and he was right to live it as he felt would be best.

Joan turned her attention to what Clara was saying. "Of course, I'd like to see you. How did you know where to find me?.......Oh yeah, that's right. When

I wasn't home, I was usually here with Grandma.....Sure, where shall I meet you?....Okay I'll be there in just a few minutes. 'Bye."

"That was Tony," Clara announced. "He's home on a two week furlough and would like me to meet him at the bus station. I said I would right away. So, guess I'd better get started. Thanks again for everything, Grandma."

Joan noticed Clara removing her engagement ring and slipping it into her purse as she turned to leave. "Come anytime, Clara," Joan said to her grand-daughter's retreating back. Looking out of the window, Joan noticed the earlier rain had stopped, and a rainbow was gleaming in the sky. "Maybe a good omen for Clara and Tony," Joan said aloud to her gray cat, Smokey, who had just entered the kitchen. "He'd be a lot better for her than Bob, I think." Except for the cat, Joan was alone. Suddenly, she felt extremely lonely. For some reason, she found herself thinking of Richard. She hadn't allowed herself to do that for a long time. In telling her story to Clara, Richard was in her thoughts and just wouldn't leave. Joan seemed to feel his presence. "Some imagination," she muttered to herself. To think of something else, she decided to fix herself a tuna and lettuce sandwich and to brew some tea.

The diversion didn't work. She couldn't seem to get Richard out of her mind. She found herself thinking of the Monday evening in November long ago when he came without phoning ahead. She'd been happy to see him, but immediately sensed something was different regarding this visit. "What's the matter, Richard?" she'd asked.

"Joannie, I can't get you out of my thoughts. I can't concentrate on my job even. That's never happened before. I'm totally and completely in love with you. It isn't going to go away. You and I need to come to an understanding. I want you in my life for as long as I live. If you feel as strongly as I do, we need to plan on getting married soon." Richard had looked pleadingly at her. "You do love me, don't you?"

Of course she did, and when Joan told him so, he held her tightly. One thing led to another and before he left that evening, Joan was wearing his ring. Both of them were very happy and "on cloud nine," as the saying goes, by the time he left well after midnight.

Another memory floated into Joan's thoughts. This time it was when Richard asked where she'd like to go to dinner. He was expecting that she'd say the name of some fancy eating establishment. Instead, Joan asked if they could go to the local pizza place. It turned out he'd never been to one. They ordered a large Hawaiian pizza and a pitcher of cold apple cider. Leftovers were taken back to Joan's house where they were eaten later that evening as they watched a black and white movie on her television screen that would seem small by today's current standards.

Lots of memories floated through Joan's mind. Time seemed to stand still, but the clock continued to count off the minutes. Soon more than an hour had passed. The doorbell rang. Thinking it was announcing the arrival of Clara and Tony, Joan smiled. Automatically, she looked in the hall mirror on her way to the front door. She patted her hair in place. She started to turn when something caught her attention in the mirror. A dim image of Smoke Man formed. He was smiling broadly at her as he pressed both of his hands together in front of his chest and bent his head in prayerful pose. It was like he was giving her a blessing and was very pleased about something. Joan blinked, and when she looked again, the image of Smoke Man was gone. Wondering what that was about, she reached the front door. She remembered she'd forgotten to lock it after Clara left. Well, it didn't matter. So sure was she that it was Clara and Tony on the porch, she didn't even check from the front window.

Joan opened the door—and standing just inside the open screen door stood Richard Seymour. *RICHARD?* Was she seeing things? His beautiful auburn hair was now gray. He'd gained weight, but he was still a handsome man. Richard noticed Joan's white hair, the loss of her young adult's curvy figure, her air of competence, and her welcoming smile!

"I'm divorced," he said before she could say anything. "I know you couldn't talk to me as long as I was married. Yes, Mrs. Phillips told me the story in the hospital the day before she passed away. She said she couldn't die with it still on her conscience. She told me in private and begged me not to tell Claudia who was unaware of what had happened. She asked me to forgive her. I took pity on her, and said I did. Can I come in?"

"Oh, sorry! Yes, do please come in." When he did, she shut the door. Joan still couldn't accept the reality of his actually being there in person, not just in her thoughts. She looked at him again and all of a sudden, it did seem real. Richard WAS there! From the look in his eyes, he still loved her. He stood looking at her, and she was staring back at him. How it happened, she didn't know, but she found herself in his arms. This was a dream come true. How—Why? What was the attraction that stayed all these years? It was more than just outer appearances. It was something that shined through his eyes—something about his inner personality that hadn't changed over the years except to become more-better was the only way she could describe it. She wondered if she and Richard were soul mates like she'd read about once in a book. Well, now wasn't the time to figure it out. He was HERE with her!

A bit later, Richard told her that he had sent Aunt Sarah a Christmas card years ago, and he'd asked her if Joan ever needed help of any kind to be sure to use the office phone he listed to let him know. Aunt Sarah had called his office after the death of Tom. She said Joan still lived in the same house she did when Richard was courting her. Aunt Sarah even gave him the number of Joan's un-listed telephone. Richard went on to say that he had driven past Joan's house a bit later and seen her in the front yard with her three children. They were plant-ing autumn bulbs beside the fence. She seemed happy with her family, and he decided to let her stay that way without interfering. Being married to Claudia and raising a son at the time made speaking his heart to Joan seem unwise. He didn't have a clue about how she might feel about him. He remembered her final letter and the later telephone conversation. He was doubtful she would respond favor-ably to anything he might say. Richard added that this was before Mrs. Phillips explained why Joan had written the letter to break their engagement and said what she did on the telephone.

Richard continued, "Yet somehow about forty-five minutes ago, I seemed to feel you thinking of me. You seemed SO close! Something echoed inside of me. Without really debating about it, I found myself in my car and driving as fast as traffic would allow. I needed to see you—and here I am! I've thought about you so many times. Just after you broke our engagement and let my family know you'd married someone else, my mother told me Claudia was pregnant by a married man. I was in a deep depression. Mother kept after me until I finally agreed that I might as well do good for somebody by helping Claudia give her baby a respectable last name. It turned out that Mrs. Phillips had lied to my mother. Claudia wasn't pregnant. I didn't discover that until after we were married. Claudia and I did have a child later. Little Christopher was a dear, and I fell in love with my son when I first held him. Claudia and I managed to get along. A little over a year ago, she told me she'd fallen in love with someone else—really deeply in love. She asked me for a divorce, and I felt relieved. Our only child was grown, married and off on his own."

"I'm glad you came, Richie. Breaking our engagement was the hardest thing I ever had to do. I suppose Mrs. Phillips told you how she convinced me to do that." Joan frowned. "You know I'd promised not to have anything to do with you as long as either of us was married because the first thing out of your mouth on the porch was the announcement of your divorce."

Richard laughed. "Quite a greeting after all these years wasn't it? Do you think we could start over, get to know each other again, and proceed to where we were when Mrs. Phillips so forcibly interfered? I'd really like the chance." He was looking into her eyes with a hopeful expression on his face.

Joan was again in his arms. "Yes, oh yes!" she told him. Somehow, she knew this time she'd end up as Mrs. Richard Seymour. Right that instant, she felt like she was probably the happiest woman on the planet—in the universe even! Richard hugged her tightly and gave her a long kiss. It was full of passion and hope. After all these years apart, they were going to have a new beginning followed by a very happy future. Joan felt elated, and she could tell Richard was happier than he could put into words.

It was then that Joan remembered Smoke Man smiling broadly and giving her a blessing judging by what she'd seen in the hall mirror on her way to answer the front door bell. She recalled his last words to her on the boat, "In the end, what is to come will meet with your approval. Be patient. Your happiness will come in time." This was the end he had promised. Her happiness was here in fuller measure than she had ever imagined could be possible.

Joan smiled and kissed Richard again.

NOTE FROM THE AUTHOR

I've written short stories. When I was in high school, a three-act play I wrote was published when my Latin II teacher was impressed enough to submit it with my permission. I'd written it for the annual Latin Club's turn to present a program for a high school assembly. I had the privilege of being Editor of my high school paper during my senior year. Over the years, some of my poems have been published, and this sometimes under the synonym of Joy Bell. *Broken Engagement-- Joan's Story* is my first novel.

This novel was written originally for my then sixth grade daughter. She'd hurry off the school bus and come rushing to me asking if I'd written more on the story. At the time, I was recovering from a nearly fatal siege of rheumatic fever. My husband purchased a portable manual typewriter for me. I'd sit up in bed propped against some pillows with the typewriter on my lap. I'd not be able to type much at first because my energy level would fail me. Yet during the day, I'd lay there and let my imagination roam regarding what to write next. It was a real morale booster.

I did copyright the story with the Library of Congress in Washington, D.C. I later deleted what seemed an unrelated sub-story and decided to call that version the Second Edition. I added some details to the story and ended up with what I copyrighted as the Third Edition. I published some copies of this to share with my special people. Recently, I found a copy stored in a box in the basement when I was looking for something else. I decided that I'd like to update the novel. I slanted it towards a more mature reader than a sixth grader. I called this the Fourth Edition. I kept upgrading the manuscript and adding more details, like the reason Mike was so interested in Joan. Adding the puppy, Woofer, brought a smile to my face. I had fun writing this story. I feel it is finally fully and completely told in this Fifth Edition.

The problem solving technique in the Epilogue reflects some of what I learned while attending group meetings of the self-help, non-profit organization called Stress Control, Inc. which was founded by the late William P. Sweet. Eventually, I became a chapter leader with that organization as well as editor of its quarterly newsletter.

My husband's pride and joy was his boat. He and I spent many happy hours on it. I enjoyed creating a boat for Mike in the story.

When I helped members of a Girl Scout patrol earn their Outdoor Cooking badges one summer, learning how to properly build a safe and effective fire was an important point. In the story, I had fun writing about the wrong way to go about starting one in a fireplace and then a better way to accomplish it.

I appreciate the helpful suggestions and technical information about particular items in the story as well as the computer help that I received from my family. My daughter, son-in-law, three sons, and two college student grandchildren all helped me in one way or another getting my story ready for publication. (Thanks to each of you!) I first published the Fifth Edition as an E-Book.

I also want to express my appreciation to the professional staff of CreateSpace (www.createspace.com) for the help given me in formatting the Fifth Edition of this novel for publication as a paperback book.

Composing *Broken Engagement--Joan's Story* has given me hours of pleasure, and I hope the reader will enjoy the result. It's nice having the time and circumstances in which I am able to continue my writing hobby. I've started a new novel. I'm grateful for my many blessing and especially for the dear people in my life.

Esther Thomson Smith